"You're my only hope..."

Angela stared at the bounty hunter's profile. Under other circumstances, she might find him mildly attractive. But now he was her captor. Her jailer. "I know you have a job to do, but this might be my only chance to prove my innocence...."

"That's not my problem."

Angela took a deep breath. She'd never stooped to feminine wiles to get anything she wanted...but she was desperate. "I...I could make it your problem...rather...worth your while."

The bounty hunter slid his glasses into his hair and narrowed his gaze at her. Blue. Micah Kaminsky's eyes were piercing blue. Angela was mesmerized for a tiny moment....

Until he asked, "Oh, yeah? How much?"

She blinked and took a deep breath to ease a vague sense of disappointment. "More than the reward for turning me in. How much would it take?"

"What makes you think I can be bought?"

Truth be known, life had taught her that almost anyone could be. "Name your price."

"What if it's too high?"

"Try me."

"What if that's my price...you?"

Dear Reader,

A hero or heroine without any faults would make pretty dull reading, since the most gripping conflicts come not from outside forces, but from within.

The Seven Deadly Sins—Pride, Sloth, Lust, Greed, Anger, Envy and Gluttony—exemplify the most hurtful behavior, human failings that can keep us locked in self-absorption and self-doubt. They can keep us from finding real happiness within ourselves...or with that one special person whom we all deserve....

As a writer, I love nothing more than throwing my heroes and heroines to the precipice of danger, making ordinary people fight the worst villains and win. For me, it's a celebration of the human spirit, the discovery of untapped strengths that I am certain we all possess if only we can find the courage to reach deep inside ourselves.

For SEVEN SINS, I've chosen to raise the stakes, to push my heroes and heroines to the emotional edge at the same time they are fighting for their very existence. In the midst of mortal danger, they must wrestle with equally destructive inner demons and take back their lives...and in doing so, be rewarded with a love for all time.

Let me know how you enjoy their stories, at P.O. Box 578279, Chicago, IL 60657-8297.

Patricia Rosemoor

Before the Fall
Patricia Rosemoor

Harlequin Books

TORONTO • NEW YORK • LONDON
AMSTERDAM • PARIS • SYDNEY • HAMBURG
STOCKHOLM • ATHENS • TOKYO • MILAN
MADRID • WARSAW • BUDAPEST • AUCKLAND

To my readers—
Thanks for your continuing support. I would love to
know which of my Intrigue titles are your favorites.

Patricia Rosemoor
P.O. Box 578297
Chicago, IL 60657-8297

ISBN 0-373-22439-7

BEFORE THE FALL

Copyright © 1997 by Patricia Pinianski

PRIDE   AVARICE

   WRATH

                    LUST

SEVEN DEADLY SINS

  ENVY

                GLUTTONY

        SLOTH

An abundance of PRIDE makes a person
    arrogant and hostile. S/he ignores
     others or hurts their feelings by
patronizing them. S/he is so competitive,
     s/he can't gracefully concede
         first place to anyone else.

CAST OF CHARACTERS

Angela Dragon (formerly Dragonetti)—The same pride that made her disown her father compelled her to prove her innocence...even if she had to break the law to do so.

Micah Kaminsky—His motives for holding Angela hostage across the country were as complicated as his feelings for her.

Tomas Dragonetti—Was Angela's recently paroled father really reformed?

Joey Mariscano—The Chicago businessman swore he had nothing to do with Angela's indictment.

Douglas Neff—The man in Angela's life stood by her...from afar.

Frank Gonnella—How nostalgic for the old days was the Las Vegas car dealer?

Otto Usher—The retired mobster had been her father's fiercest rival. Was he carrying the feud on to the next generation?

Leon Woerter—The bail bondsman was in the right place at the right time.

Prologue

Alex Gotham planted himself before the turn-of-the-century Dupont Circle mansion and flipped a coin. Heads, he would go inside. Tails, he would get his butt back where it belonged.

Heads.

Brushing aside his reservations, he entered the brick-and-sandstone building that now housed Haven, a privately funded mental health foundation. Not unaware of the irony of his reason for being there, Alex strolled through the lobby with its fluted Ionic oak columns and ascended the curving staircase to Zoe Declue's office.

He'd never actually spoken to the research psychologist. She'd left a phone message asking him if he'd be willing to collaborate on a project—after considering all the angles, he'd made an appointment through her secretary. From Zoe's formal, no-nonsense message, he'd gotten the impression of a mature woman, so he was naturally surprised when he came face-to-face with a lovely blonde who couldn't have been much older than thirty.

"Mr. Gotham. I hope you don't mind if I call you Alex." Her voice low and silky, she added, "I'm delighted to meet you at last. Thank you for coming."

When she leaned across her desk to give him her hand, he noticed that the chin-length cornsilk hair that swept across her cheeks did hold a sheen of silver. Her shake was solid and yet a touch reserved—as was her expression. Her welcoming smile didn't quite light her deep green eyes...as if she were as wary of him as he was of her. Her cautious demeanor made her seem older than her years.

"I'm curious about this Seven Deadly Sins project of yours," Alex admitted. Which her message hadn't explained in any detail. She'd merely stated she wanted to reach a large audience and felt that her own writing was too academic. "And curious as to why you contacted *me*."

"Please...sit."

Awash in textured whites and creams with pale touches of flesh and peach, the office seemed to be a reflection of the woman herself—cool and controlled, yet hinting of a subdued sensuality. He chose a chair upholstered in nubby cream and satiny ivory stripes. She remained behind her desk.

"When I realized I needed a collaborator," she began, "your book *Lost Youth* immediately came to mind. A very powerful piece of nonfiction. You took me inside each of those teenagers. You made me understand their despairs and their hopes. You made me feel for them...and maybe learn a few things about myself."

"I'm flattered." Though Alex couldn't fathom what Zoe Declue might possibly have in common with a runaway kid.

"I feel you have the right touch...not only the insight, but the sensitivity to people that I'm looking for."

Or he'd had it once, Alex thought ruefully.

Lost Youth had briefly cast a moderately known investigative reporter, whose primary focus had been the root of social ills, into the universe of bright new stars in the publishing world. Too soon, however, his life had taken a gruesome turn for which he hadn't been prepared. He'd taken one wrong step after another...his star had fizzled...his very existence had imploded into a black hole. Now he was ready to glue back together the pieces of his life...given the right opportunity.

Wondering if he still had the touch, he asked, "What kind of an approach did you have in mind?"

"Humanistic rather than theological. I intend to explore each of the Seven Deadly Sins—Pride, Envy, Wrath, Sloth, Avarice, Gluttony and Lust—as to how they relate to today's world."

She seemed so solemn that Alex couldn't resist asking, "And you need someone to help you do the personal research?"

Obviously thrown, Zoe started, then stared at him as if she weren't sure how to take the droll comment. Alex silently cursed. He'd have to watch himself around her. Thankfully, she recouped and indicated a stack of near-bursting files at the side of her desk.

"I've already gathered research from colleagues across the country," she informed him. "The subjects have agreed to share their stories—how they wrestled with their demons and won. Anonymously, of course."

"Stories?"

Nodding, she kept a wary eye on him. "One to examine each of the sins, which I believe are emotion-based and keep a person isolated from society...and therefore from loving freely. Only by resolving the sin against him- or herself and really connecting with others can that person find fulfillment and happiness."

As she got caught up in her topic, Alex was struck by

her expression—as if she were looking inward, searching for some truth about self.

Suddenly uneasy, he murmured, "Stories about people giving themselves a second chance at life." What he himself needed.

"Exactly. I want to help people recognize the trouble they attract and offer them hope that they can change and lead more fulfilling lives. And happier ones."

Again Alex had the fleeting impression of a personal interest in the topic. He knew *he* felt it personally. Maybe too much so to be objective?

Then again, who hadn't sinned?

He needed the work, he rationalized, and so asked, "How do we begin?"

Zoe reached toward the middle of her desk for what looked like a legal contract. "I've worked out an agreement—"

"Skip the technicalities for now." He didn't want to discuss money, either, though his bank account was sagging—ever since he'd blown his job at the *Washington Sun,* freelance assignments had been few and far between. More important was finding a way to recover his sense of self. "I meant the content."

Nodding, she shifted her attention to the top of the stack and lifted the first thick file. From the folder spilled original articles and copies and handwritten notes.

"Let me talk you through the first chapter, while you have a look at the materials I've collected. Then you decide whether or not the project interests you enough to throw yourself into it." Warming to her subject, she loosened up. "Our subject is Angela Dragon. Actually, that was Dragonetti before she legally changed it on her eighteenth birthday."

"Dragonetti?" he echoed as she handed him a clipping.

His investigative reporter's antennae raised by the notorious name, he read the headline: *Mobster's Daughter Indicted...*

Chapter One

"This sucks the big one," Angela Dragon muttered under her breath while storming out of the courtroom.

Her high heels clacked briskly against the marble floor. Surrounded by her lawyer, her father, the rest of her family and the man she was currently seeing, she put up a good front as members of the press rushed her.

Smile. Show those pearly whites. Don't let a bunch of reporters desperate to get a story whip you.

A determined young woman shoved a microphone practically in her face. "Miss Dragon, did you expect to be indicted?"

"Is there any truth to the charges?" asked a buck-toothed man on her other side. "And is your father involved?"

"Why don't you ask *me* if that's what you want to know?" Tomas Dragonetti suggested coldly.

A third reporter assailed her with "Do you really want us to believe you could buy a photo and video company not knowing it was a front for a pornographic operation and a cover for money-laundering activities?"

Angela lifted her chin and was about to give the little snot a blistering retort when her lawyer, Mark Jenkins, growled, "Don't do it."

And on her other side, her sister, Petra, dug her nails into her arm. "Angela, please."

Controlling her temper, she whispered through gritted teeth, "All right!"

They plowed through the viper's nest and out into late-afternoon sunshine even more brilliant than Angela's jonquil yellow suit, then raced down the courthouse steps to the waiting limousine. A welcome breeze skittered over Angela, fluttering the heavy, shoulder-length hair that was her pride. She pushed the mass of natural waves out of her eyes and took a deep breath of dry desert air.

Such a beautiful day to have one's life ruined.

Despite her outward belligerence toward the legal system and the media, Angela was shaking inside. Not that she would ever show weakness—lest she be eaten alive by the hordes of eager reporters.

"We're going to get through this, darling."

Looking into Douglas Neff's hazel eyes as he helped her into the back seat of the limo, she grabbed at the reassurance. "Of course we are."

He slid in next to her and dipped his head, brushing her lips with his mustache. She forced a smile. With his classic good looks and perfect tan, and his impeccably cut Armani suit, Douglas was a man many a woman would sigh over. Not that *she* was a woman who ever sighed...or believed in romantic claptrap. Look where her mother's stalwart devotion to her father had gotten them. But, a successful financial adviser who respected her intelligence and abilities and refused to be intimidated by her drive, Douglas was the first man she'd dated who had a real possibility of becoming more to her than a convenient escort.

Staunchly shifting in her seat next to her husband, her

mother, Sylvie, assured her, "Your family's behind you, sweetheart."

Exactly what Angela feared. She didn't need—or want—her father's involvement. But despite the fact that Angela had never accepted his return to the fold the way the rest of the family had since his parole six months before, Tomas Dragonetti wouldn't let her forget that he was her father and that he supposedly loved her.

A love she could certainly do without.

"I'm gonna get to the truth if it's the last thing I ever do," her father muttered. "Whoever set up my baby won't get away with this."

What was he going to do? Angela wondered. Have the guilty one rubbed out?

She shuddered at the very idea of violence.

If only Benedict were here.

She'd always been able to count on her older brother for emotional support. And he'd know what to do, how to get her out of this mess. But, having chosen to leave the running of Here Comes the Bride to her, he was off building his career in middle Europe, and she hadn't wanted to drag him home to this mess.

"I want you *all* to stay out of it," she announced, her determined gaze burning into her father's face.

With his history, he could instigate additional trouble for the family. Her mother certainly didn't need more grief. And the youngest of the siblings, Petra, had always been sheltered. She was a true innocent, and Angela hoped her sister's faith in human nature would never be shattered the way her own had been.

"What do you mean, stay out of it?" Douglas asked. "We're in this together. You bought Picture Perfect with my encouragement. I feel responsible."

"Well, don't." Angela refused to involve a man who

had no underworld connections…other than her via her own father. Besides, she didn't feel close enough to Douglas to be totally open and honest.

"I have an investigator already working on the case," Jenkins added.

"Hiring an investigator's fine. But I'm a big girl. I got myself into trouble." *How* was just now beginning to dawn on her. "I'll damn well get myself out." Her pride wouldn't let her do less than she could.

"And how do you think you'll manage that, Angel?" her father asked.

Hating it when he used his childhood nickname for her, she stared at him. Voice stiff, she said, "As you keep reminding me, I *am* your daughter."

Once a prominent Las Vegas mobster, Tomas had been in control of his little corner of the world until it had been ripped from his hands by the authorities. *That* she had inherited from him—the lust for control over her own life and the determination not to let go without a fight.

She was innocent of the charges brought against her, and she would damn well prove it to everyone's satisfaction. Even the D.A.'s.

"WHAT ARE YOU UP TO, Angela?" Douglas demanded a while later, pouring them glasses of brandy.

He'd insisted on coming home with her against her wishes. It wasn't that she didn't appreciate his concern, but she didn't choose to explain herself to anyone. The less others knew about the plan that had been fomenting in her head all the way home, the safer they would be.

Besides, if they didn't know anything, they wouldn't be able to give her grief.

Or try to stop her.

As Douglas handed her a glass and slid next to her on the red leather couch, Angela said, "I'm going to finish this drink and get some rest," hoping he would take the hint.

"I know you better than that. I can hear the wheels turning in that pretty head of yours."

Sipping the brandy, she waited for the warmth to fill her—to calm her nerves—before saying, "I was just trying to figure out who might have it in for me."

Who would want to take her away from everything she knew? From the people she loved? The work that had become her life's blood? The two-story condo whose decor reflected the complexity of her mind, the impetuousness of her spirit?

"And?" Douglas pressed. "Have you come up with a suspect?"

"I'm not sure."

"But you can make an educated guess."

She debated the wisdom of telling him, then figured sharing something as simple as a name and a little background couldn't hurt in case something went awry. "Joey Mariscano."

"Who?"

"A businessman from out of town who paid me a visit a while back. He suggested it would be in my best interests to let him and his 'associates' buy into Here Comes the Bride. I suggested he take the first plane back to Chicago. He wasn't happy with my refusal, intimated I would regret my decision. At the time, I figured he meant I'd regret turning down bigger profits."

"You never said anything to me about this."

"It happened before we met. Several weeks, I think." And they'd been seeing each other for more than three months. "I guess that's why I didn't think of him right away."

Douglas swirled his brandy. "What do you guess he wanted exactly?"

"I'm not certain, but my father had been paroled a short while before. Maybe Mariscano assumed Father had taken more than a passing—and legal—interest in the family business. I suppose he figured he would do well to get in on the action while I was still in charge."

Not that she would ever let her father near Here Comes the Bride.

After Tomas Dragonetti had been incarcerated—his business interests, property and investments all confiscated by the government—his wife had needed to find a means of support for her three children. Quiet, delicate Sylvie Dragonetti had sold off property she'd inherited from her parents and had used the money to start a bridal-wear shop. As the wedding capital of the world, Las Vegas couldn't have too many of those.

Angela had been fifteen at the time, Benedict seventeen, while Petra had been nine—only a kid. Angela and Benedict had protected Petra from the ugly truth as best they could. They'd also worked alongside their mother every chance they had.

What else did they have to do with their free time after everyone they knew deserted them because of their father?

Ostracized and humiliated, Angela had vowed that someday she'd show the world the stuff of which she was made. She'd also sworn never to trust anyone but her mother and siblings and had devoted herself to them and the company. After college, even knowing he'd wanted to turn his end of the business over to her and find a niche for himself in computer software, she'd sucked Benedict into helping her expand. Over the past decade, one bridal shop had become three. After which, they'd built their own wedding chapel. Started their own limousine service. Bought out a successful flower shop, which Petra now ran. Then, two years ago, Benedict finally left Here Comes the Bride for new challenges that were his own rather than hers.

And Angela had been left in a position of sole control...which included taking responsibility if anything went wrong. Now she was facing the possibility of going to jail for something about which she hadn't had a clue.

How could this have happened to her?

Douglas intruded on her thoughts. "Have you told anyone else about Mariscano?"

"Not yet," she hedged, hoping he would believe she meant to.

"You should get Jenkins's investigator on it."

"You're absolutely right."

But Angela wasn't planning on involving anyone else in this investigation if she didn't have to. Certain she could manipulate Mariscano into spilling his guts if only she had the opportunity, Angela was plotting a face-to-face meeting with the rat—as soon as possible. At the moment, only Douglas stood in her way.

Yawning, she said, "About that nap..."

He stroked her hair tenderly. "I wouldn't mind holding you in my arms until you fall asleep."

Considering the disastrous state of her life at the moment, Angela wasn't about to start a new phase in their relationship. Nor would she let herself be distracted from her purpose. "I'd rather be alone, if you don't mind."

He did mind. His expression told her so. But Douglas was a true gentleman. He pretended he didn't and left without a fuss, promising to call her promptly at noon the next day. She smiled and murmured noon would be fine, all the time knowing that she wouldn't be available.

She'd already be in Chicago.

Making haste to pack an overnight bag, Angela tried not to dwell on the fact that by crossing the state line, she would knowingly break the law.

OBLIVIOUS to the impending dawn, Micah Kaminsky stretched out on his bed and groaned in ecstasy. Finally he was going to get some much-needed rest, delayed by his latest job. The badly worn mattress might have lost some of its spring, but Micah was tired enough for it to feel like he was floating on a cloud. He was fast zeroing in on the twilight zone when the telephone shattered the silence and jarred his eyes open. Muttering a curse, he pulled a pillow over his head and let the damn thing ring.

Eventually, the answering machine would pick up....

Only it didn't.

And the telephone refused to shut up.

Irritated, he grabbed the receiver and growled, "This better be important!"

"If it wasn't, I wouldn't be bothering you."

Immediately recognizing the voice, Micah made an attempt to concentrate as the man on the other end called in a long-overdue favor.

"She goes by 'Angela Dragon,'" the man continued, "though she used some alias to book her flight. She's on her way to Chicago now."

"Jumped bail, huh? Not too bright."

"Don't underestimate her, Kaminsky. She's damned smart and she'll fight you tooth and nail. Do whatever is necessary to get her back to Las Vegas pronto. Agreed?"

"Done. We both know I'm in your debt."

"This'll square things between us."

Good. Micah hated owing anyone anything. Listening to a detailed description of the woman in addition to other pertinent information, he forced himself back up to his feet, his only regret having to abandon the siren song of his bed yet again. Stretching, he smothered a yawn. A pot of coffee would be in order before leaving for the airport to intercept the woman. He needed a clear head. Not that he felt especially challenged by the assignment.

Compared to the jobs he'd executed lately, getting a headstrong woman back where she belonged would be a piece of cake.

NOON CAME AND WENT before Angela pulled the rental car in to the McCormick Place parking lot. She couldn't stop peering over her shoulder.

Though she hoped she'd been imagining it—courtesy of a guilty conscience over leaving Nevada illegally—she'd had the weirdest sensation of being followed, first from the airport to Mariscano's home, then from the North Shore suburb to the convention complex. Every so often, in her rearview window, she'd gotten sight of an older-model dark coupe cruising some distance behind. There was a good probability that she'd actually spotted several different cars similar in style, but she hadn't wanted to take any chances. She'd done some fancy driving and had gone miles out of her way to lose any possible tail.

Her paranoia taking up enough time so that she'd missed Joey Mariscano by minutes.

A fair acting job on her part convinced the housekeeper that she had important business with the man.

The woman had acknowledged that her employer wouldn't be home all day—he was escorting his newly engaged daughter DeeDee to a bridal exposition.

So here she was, home away from home. She couldn't count the number of similar showings she'd attended for new ideas and products over the years. She'd even been to this particular event more than once in the past few years and was personally acquainted with several of the major vendors.

As she started to proceed to the center on foot, a flash from the corner of her eye prompted her to glance around the parking lot. A midnight blue car pulled in to a vacant spot in the next row. The same vehicle that she'd imagined had been following her? She hesitated, waiting to see who got out, but the driver didn't seem to be in any hurry to leave the car. Shaking away her trepidation, she started off, alert to the possibility of trouble. But none materialized.

Inside, the crowded lobby rang with excited female voices and seventies music played by a DJ for hire. Once equipped with an official pass, Angela wondered where to start. She couldn't feature Joey Mariscano scouring the vendor area, where booth aisles were choked with thousands of women pawing over naughty lingerie, devouring tidbits from various caterers or comparing travel agents for the best honeymoon package.

Checking the special-events list, she noted that a bridal fashion show featuring several exclusive designers would begin in half an hour. This particular event meant primarily for buyers wasn't generally open to the public, though an individual with clout could obtain a pass.

And she'd bet anything Joey Mariscano had clout.

As she was about to follow her instincts, a prickling sensation at the back of her neck made her hesitate. Had the shady businessman found her first? Tightening her jaw, Angela lifted her chin and turned around.

The man who was staring at her from a distance was definitely not Joey Mariscano. At least, she thought he was staring. Hard to tell what those eyes were doing on the other side of his mirrored sunglasses.

As for the rest of him, all six feet plus was on alert, though he was evidently trying for a casual pose, shoulder wedged against a pillar. The deep blue T-shirt that showed off his impressive musculature was a bit casual for the event. And beard stubbled his strong jawline, while golden brown hair too long to be in vogue splayed across his high forehead and broad cheeks. His rumpled appearance suggested that he'd just gotten out of bed.

And perhaps he had, she thought, flushing.

Figuring he was a flirtatious bridegroom-to-be, Angela took pity on the woman who would marry him, shook off the odd feeling he aroused in her and rushed toward the hall set up for the fashion show. Flashing her pass, she stepped inside. Nearly full already.

How would she ever find the man she was pursuing?

Logic told her he would command one of the best seats in the house, as close as possible to the merchandise. Her gaze traveled along the temporary runway…stopping at a broad back covered by a navy blue suit that might be expensive but that was also a half size too small. She'd recognize that chunky body anywhere. And he was talking with both ring-bedecked hands waving.

Joey Mariscano's size hadn't changed…nor his vanity.

Smiling, Angela murmured, "Gotcha!" then appraised the situation and impetuously formulated a daring plan.

"LISTEN, DARLING, my lady is one of the models," Micah smoothly lied to the pretty young redhead at the door.

"She should have given you a pass."

He cocked his sunglasses up into his hair and crinkled his eyes at her. For some reason, women always responded well to that.

"She was supposed to leave me a pass, but we got up late. Know what I mean? She was in such a hurry to get out of the apartment that she plumb forgot...."

"Uh, I suppose it won't hurt anything...." Color creeping into her cheeks, the young woman looked around as if to make certain they weren't being watched. "Go on in. Hurry."

Micah didn't waste any time. He slipped into a seat at the back of the hall and scanned the room for a brunette in a bloodred suit with black trim.

He'd been told Angela Dragon was a looker. No exaggeration there, he thought, reflecting on the woman he'd just caught sight of at the airport. Slightly tilted almond-shaped dark eyes. Narrow nose, high cheekbones and hollow cheeks framed by lush dark hair. Lips full enough to tempt a man. And with those long, long legs and waist small enough to encircle with his hands, she really could be a model.

Angela Dragon would stand out in any crowd... only...not this one.

For, try as he might, he couldn't place her. Worried that this time she really had lost him—she'd driven erratically all morning as if she'd had reason to suspect she was being followed—he cursed to himself. He should have snatched her from Mariscano's property, no matter that the elderly woman next door was paying closer attention to Angela's doings than to her gardening.

He hadn't wanted any witnesses. No need to call attention to his actions. He'd meant to wait to get her alone...but now he worried that she'd given him the slip and he might not get her at all.

Thinking about the possibility of having to admit failure made him wince inside.

"VIDA, YOU'RE A LOVE. I'll never forget you for this," Angela told the designer whose line of bridal fashions sold like hotcakes for Here Comes the Bride.

The other woman clucked to herself as she fussed with the material. "I still really don't understand why you want to do this."

Angela hadn't been too specific. She'd merely asked for the favor and had said it was important to her.

"All right," she said. "To give a certain man in the audience the surprise of his life."

Wasn't that the truth!

A knowing expression softened Vida's exotic Eastern European features. "Ah, the light dawns." She tapped her forehead with her palm. "I am so stupid. No, *he* is the stupid one for not marrying you already."

Cringing inside at her deception, promising herself she'd make it all up to the designer later, Angela hugged the smaller woman. "Thank you."

"No need for thanks. Such a romantic gesture makes my heart flutter," Vida said with her usual drama. "Why else would I be in this business?"

"Why else, indeed?" Angela echoed, her realistic nature silently answering *For the money, of course.*

"When your lover sees you looking so radiant, how will he resist proposing?"

"He'd *better* not resist me," Angela murmured as she turned to the mirror for a final check. She couldn't wait to see Joey Mariscano's face when he recognized her.

Hardly recognizing herself, she stared in surprise. Flushed with excitement, she looked exactly like a radiant bride in a cream-colored creation embellished with handmade lace, silk rosebuds, Austrian crystals and seed pearls. The full bustle and train added to the cut of the garment emphasized the smallness of her waist and the fullness of her breasts.

And the matching lace veil secured with several large bobby pins to the loose dark curls gathered at the top of her head—hair tamed courtesy of Vida's stylist, despite the wretched Midwestern humidity—would hide her features until it was too late for the crook to make his getaway.

NERVES STRUCK HER as Angela stepped onto the runway and into view of the crowd. But the "oohs" and "aahs" of the audience reassured her. They were concentrating on the dress. Not on her. No one suspected a thing.

She swept down the length of the runway even as she'd seen it done thousands of times. The classical music beneath the announcer's voice helped keep her calm. Passing the model making her way back, Angela twirled gracefully, glad the only pair of available heels they could find to fit her were far lower than her own. She needed to keep her equilibrium, she thought, stopping directly in front of Joey Mariscano and his daughter—a pretty young thing, her hopes for the future reflected in her beaming smile.

Angela swallowed hard. Poor DeeDee. Her day was about to be ruined...if not her image of her father. She certainly could empathize.

Through the veil's lace she stared at Mariscano with his dyed-black hair and full jowls. He wasn't even looking at her. The focus of his attention, his daughter wore almost as much gold jewelry as the father.

Angela gritted her teeth at the crook's loving expression for his child...the same as she'd seen on her own father's face.

Distracted, she lost her momentum. But only for a moment. Then she finished her tour of the stage and stepped down into the audience, where other models were gliding along various aisles, giving buyers a closer look at the goods.

The audience's attention shifted to the next model, and Angela went straight for her target. She stopped directly in front of him, blocking his view of the stage.

"Joey, we need to talk." She lifted the veil. "In private."

She saw instant recognition flare in his eyes before he covered it with a mask of polite confusion. "Excuse me?"

"Daddy, who is this woman?"

"No one, sweetheart." Expression blank, he said, "You mistake me for someone else. We're here to find a dress for my daughter's wedding."

Angela turned this way and that, pretending to be modeling for an interested customer. "And I'm here to clear up a few things between us."

The daughter gasped. "She isn't one of your *women,* for heaven's sake, is she? You're not going to invite her to the *wedding,* are you?"

"She's no one—"

Angela bristled. "My *name* is Angela Dragon." Lifting an eyebrow, she gave Mariscano a haughty glare. "Not exactly no one."

She forgot what she'd been about to say when a hulking form rose behind father and daughter. Broad as a bear, he appeared equally mean, the corner of one narrowed eye distorted by a nasty scar. His lips thinned in an imitation of a smile.

"Mr. Mariscano, you want I should take care of this situation for you?" he growled.

"I am not a situation," Angela countered.

"No. Sit, Adolpho."

His grimace telegraphing his disappointment, Adolpho sat on command. A well-trained bear, Angela decided, noting that heads were turning in their direction and that Mariscano seemed a bit uneasy. Good for her.

"As for you, Miss...uh, Dragon, is it?...if you wanna talk to me, call my office for an appointment." He held out his card. "Tell my secretary I said to find some time for you."

She ignored the card. "Time is exactly what I don't have...as you well know." At least, she was pretty certain he did, Angela thought, hoping she wasn't making a fool of herself. What if Mariscano really *didn't* know anything? For a moment she wavered. Better a fool than convicted without trying to clear her name, she thought. Aware of the interest of patrons around them, she said, "We need to talk *now*. I suggest we step out into the hall."

"Daddy," DeeDee whispered frantically, "you didn't get *this one* pregnant, did you?"

"Of course not, baby," he reassured her, patting her hand. With a steely expression aimed at Angela, he said, "I ain't goin' nowhere."

"Then neither am I." Angela raised the volume a notch, hoping the possibility of embarrassing his daughter would make Mariscano fold.

"Oh, yes, you are," came a deep-timbred voice as a large hand gripped her upper arm and spun her around.

Angela widened her eyes the second they connected with the mirrored sunglasses topping her by several inches. "You!" she gasped. Another of Mariscano's bodyguards?

"C'mon." He tugged on her arm. "Don't make a scene or you'll be sorry."

The threat fueled Angela's easily ignited temper. She wasn't about to go anywhere with him. Digging in, she ordered, "Take your hand off my arm!"

"Okay."

But no sooner did he release his firm grip than he dipped his head and butted his right shoulder into her solar plexus, knocking the breath out of her. His arms wrapped around the back of her legs and he straightened. In a flash, her world turned upside down.

Using a fireman's carry, the stranger hauled her away from the stage.

Chapter Two

Angela was so stunned at his audacity that for a moment she couldn't react. The blackguard had her halfway toward the exit before she demanded, "Put me down!" and, for emphasis, whacked him in the middle of the back.

"I wouldn't do that again," he warned.

Angela took the challenge. She whacked him a second time, then went speechless when he responded in kind, her derriere being his target. Considering how strong he was—she was definitely no lightweight, and, besides, she'd noted his impressive musculature in the lobby earlier—she was thankful for the protective padding provided by the full bustle.

Determined to free herself before he could get her alone, she struggled, but the elaborate wedding dress held her nearly as fast as his arms. If she could only get down to her feet, she could handle herself using what she'd learned in her college self-defense class. Of course, more than a decade had since slipped by, but she was confident the moves would all come back to her. It would be just like riding a bicycle—no one ever forgot how to do that. Try as she might, though, she couldn't budge him.

Adding insult to injury, people on both sides of the aisle found her predicament amusing. Nervous coughs and snickers set her further on edge. Undoubtedly, they assumed this travesty was all part of the fashion show.

"Someone help me!" she demanded, lifting her head and glaring through the double layer of veil that had flopped over her face. "I don't even know this man!" When someone laughed outright, she flushed with humiliation. "Go ahead and amuse yourselves. For all you know, he could be a killer!" The words flew from her lips unbidden.

Titters followed them straight out the door.

And still he didn't let her down.

Rather than turning toward the lobby, he headed in the opposite direction, away from the crowd. *Killer* echoed through her mind. What if he was? A few people lingered in the hallway. Surely *someone* would take her seriously. But when she pleaded for help next, a trio of women merely stared openmouthed. And farther along, a grandfatherly type issued encouragement to her abductor.

"That's it, bucko," he called after them with a chuckle. "Show her who's boss *before* the wedding."

"This is no joke!" she shouted, only to see the bozo nearly collapse with laughter.

That's when she noticed they were exiting through a rear door meant for use by the trades. They were in a stairwell, and her captor was shooting down the metal steps. Realizing this was a great place to commit murder without anyone being the wiser, Angela tried not to panic. Surely if Joey Mariscano had wanted her dead, he would have hired someone in Nevada to rub her out rather than set her up.

But that was before she'd made a scene in front of his precious DeeDee....

Spotting an exposed pipe, she latched on to it and hung on for dear life. Her abductor merely paused, grunted and put extra might into his next step.

Angela yelped when her hands ripped free. Her fingers burned as if he'd set them on fire. And, pummeled by his shoulder, her stomach ached. Hanging topsy-turvy while descending the stairs generated a queasy sensation and a light head. She was not in top form.

"You'd better put me down before I throw up all over you," she threatened.

"You do, and I'll put you down, all right. I'll drop you on your head."

Uttering a raw sound of frustration, Angela went for *his* head, the automatic response reminiscent of childhood fights with Benedict. Both hands filled with her abductor's hair, she pulled as hard as she could... considering her awkward position and the hindrance caused by the wedding dress and too-tight corset beneath. She'd tear his damn hair out by the roots if she could!

All she got for her valiant effort was a low grunt. Having reached the next landing, he opened the door to the outside. She let go. Several strands of golden brown hair clung to her fingers. She shook them away in distaste.

Once more, Angela tried to save herself by hooking on to the edge of the steel panel. An ineffectual effort. Even as her hands popped free, a breeze fluttered the lace veil into the door's hardware. Though she heard a slight tearing sound, the material held fast. Her abductor kept going, and she imagined her own hair being ripped from her scalp.

"Wait a minute. Stop! Ouch!" she shrieked, the veil finally freeing itself from her head, a dark curl still attached to the lace via a bobby pin. "Oh, my God, my hair!" Frantically she searched for the bare patch as he swung around for a look.

Then he snorted. "Serves you right for trying to pull out mine."

Damn him! He loses a few strands of hair and for that she's rewarded with a bald spot. Actually, the area was half the size of a dime, but it felt like a crater to her trembling fingers. Seeing-red angry, she sought revenge.

For the next hundred feet or so, she used every point of attack she could think of to free herself. She kicked at him, but his grip around her thighs was so tight she couldn't get enough leverage to make more than surface contact. When she clawed at his back, he wormed around as if she were scratching an itch for him. She aimed for his face, but he caught her already abused fingers firmly between his teeth.

Clenching her jaw so she wouldn't cry out, Angela waited for the pain. When none came, she shrewdly pulled her hand away.

"Are you done?" he asked so calmly that she wanted to scream.

"Are *you?* If so, you can release me." She waited a beat and asked, "What are your plans for me?"

He chose not to answer, making her very, very nervous.

Maybe Mariscano *had* had a change of heart and wanted her dead.

She gazed around at the sea of cars for other people. Not everyone would take her abduction as a joke. But the parking lot was free of pedestrians, and her hopes for outside assistance shattered. As usual, she had to rely on herself. She took a big, calming breath and tried to dredge up some of those self-defense techniques. The blackguard would have to set her down eventually, and she wanted to be ready to take him on.

Suddenly he stopped.

Not having counted on her head going light when he righted her, a disoriented Angela swayed and fought to find her bearings. She had hardly got a glimpse of the midnight blue car—the same dark vehicle that had been following her, no doubt—when he propelled her inside.

Landing in the lumpy passenger seat of the old Thunderbird, she protested, "Oh, no, you don't!"

"I already have."

She tried to make a break, but her legs tangled in the yards and yards of her skirt. The rusty bottom of the door slammed on the train, leaving a trail of material outside the car. Horrified, she gaped, but quickly found her wits. While her abductor jogged around to the other side, she grabbed the door handle. The latch lifted but nothing happened.

He slid into the driver's seat. "Try all you want. You won't get out unless I release your lock."

"What? You do this sort of thing frequently enough to have the equipment modified?"

"Let's say I appreciate all aspects of security." He started the engine. "Buckle up."

Knowing she was stuck, Angela pulled the belt across her chest and fastened it. Force hadn't freed her. Maybe calm logic would.

If he responded to logic. He wasn't like any man she'd ever known. He seemed uncivilized yet absolutely focused. Intense and a little scary.

She stole a sideways glance, noting that everything about him seemed larger than life. Her gaze slid from shoulders to arms to the hands gripping the steering wheel. The hands presented a puzzling contradiction in and of themselves. While they appeared as powerful as the rest of him, the fingers were long and tapered like the tools of a musician or an artist rather than those of a thug or killer.

Then again, the man himself presented yet another puzzling contradiction. He didn't come off as unintelligent...or as someone who would take orders without question. Not like his counterpart Adolpho.

Try logic, definitely, she told herself, and said, "Mariscano's overreacting."

"To what?"

"To my simply wanting to talk to him."

He pulled out of the parking space and headed the vehicle toward the exit. "Talk? You were ordering him around. Seems to come naturally to you."

Angela swallowed hard and told herself to keep her temper in check. "He wasn't taking my request seriously." She put on an ingenuous face. "He'll regret this later, so it doesn't make sense to act rashly now. I didn't mean him any harm," she fibbed. Unless she was mistaken about Mariscano's involvement, she meant to see the crooked businessman's butt behind bars, and he would definitely consider a stretch in the pen a threat to his mental health. "Really."

He shrugged. "Okay, if you say so."

"Then you'll let me go?"

"Nope."

"Why not? Where are you taking me? What are you going to do to me? Did Mariscano give you orders to fit me with a pair of cement overshoes?"

She shot her questions at him in rapid fire without bothering to hide her sarcasm.

His mirrored gaze traveled over her. Slowly.

"Cement shoes wouldn't go with the party dress."

For a moment his biting return stiffened Angela's spine. Then she realized she was in hot water for yet another infraction.

The bridal gown!

Angela glanced down to where the train was caught in the door. "Oh, my god, Vida will have a fit if she doesn't get this back. I hope it isn't ruined." She could imagine the delicate material shredding as it swept the street. "Do you have any idea what this designer original is worth?"

"Not a clue."

"More than you're making for whatever it is you plan to do with me."

As he turned the car onto Lake Shore Drive, he said, "I'm making sure you get back to Las Vegas."

"Pardon me?" After the way he'd manhandled her, she could hardly believe he didn't have more dastardly plans in mind. "That's all Mariscano asked you to do? To see that I get on a plane headed for home?"

"A train."

"Train?" she echoed, suddenly puzzled.

"And I'm escorting you all the way."

The thought of remaining in the brute's company for however long it took to get cross-country—at least a whole day, she was certain—was unsettling. "I don't get it."

"Seems there's a lot you don't get," he said wryly. "I'm not a hit man. And I would never work for the likes of Joey Mariscano."

The last stopped her cold. So she'd been wrong, but what else was she to have assumed? Who then had sent him chasing after her? The person who'd set her up...as in someone *other than* Mariscano? Angela wondered if she could worm the information out of him.

"So what's your interest?" she asked.

"You skipped a state line."

The unexpected answer startled her. She pulled a face. "You're a *bounty hunter?*"

"Micah Kaminsky," he said, with a tip of his head.

Great! Now she was in *big* trouble. The law was involved.

How had this happened? she wondered as they raced along Lake Michigan, museums straight ahead reaching out into the waters. Who'd figured out where she was headed? And for that matter, how could anyone have known for certain that she'd skipped out of town?

Someone must have been keeping an eye on her.

And she would be in trouble *whenever* she returned. It wouldn't be now, though, not without putting up a fight. She was sticking with her Mariscano theory, and Mariscano was here. Physically exhausted, however, she didn't see how she could win any struggle against Kaminsky's strength.

Angela stared openly at the bounty hunter's Eastern European profile, especially the pronounced nose, slightly flattened cheeks and strong jawline. Under other circumstances, she might think him mildly attractive rather than brutish. But he was her captor, she reminded herself. Her jailer.

Back to business—scrutinizing him for some sign of weakness.

At first sight in the lobby, she'd thought him sleep rumpled. Closer inspection prompted a reevaluation. Beneath the beard stubble his face was drawn, especially at the corners of the wide mouth that framed so many annoying comments. He appeared tired. Exhausted, even. If so, he couldn't be all that sharp mentally.

Maybe she could convince him to delay their departure...tire him out even more...watch for him to let down his guard...then escape.

Angela stared out at the lake longingly. If only she were skimming the surface on one of those boats whose sails filled with the wind. For that matter, a speedboat would do. Or any form of transportation that would take her as far away from Micah Kaminsky as was possible.

"Would it make any difference if I told you I was innocent?" she asked.

"That's the beauty of our legal system—everyone's innocent until proven guilty."

"And that's what I'm trying to prevent from happening. Being found guilty." She burned her gaze into him. "Someone set me up, most likely Joey Mariscano."

"And you simply wanted to talk to him about it."

"Exactly."

They were delayed by a red light. He turned toward her and gave her a pitying look. At least, she thought so—the sunglasses were still intact.

"You figure some crook would spill his guts because a gorgeous woman bats her eyes at him?"

"I never said it would be that easy. And I don't *eye-bat*," she informed him, not deaf to the reference about her being gorgeous.

She'd never stooped to using feminine wiles to get anything she wanted, either in her professional or in her personal life, and she wasn't about to break that sterling record.

"With a little quality time," she continued, "I might have been able to get the truth out of him. I still might if I were free to take a stab at it."

"Right. And Mariscano would willingly turn himself in to the authorities to clear your name."

Having been so focused on wringing a confession out of the crook, she hadn't planned her next step. But if she could only get confirmation that Mariscano wanted to take her down because she wouldn't cooperate in his slimy deal, she'd find a way to prove it to the authorities.

"I know you have a job to do, but try to see things from my perspective," she said. "This might be my only chance to prove my innocence."

"That's not my problem."

"I could make it your problem...rather...worth your while."

He slid the sunglasses into his hair and narrowed his gaze at her. Blue. Kaminsky's eyes were piercing blue. Angela was mesmerized for a tiny moment...

Until he asked, "Oh, yeah? How much?"

She blinked and took a deep breath to ease a vague sense of disappointment. "More than the reward for turning me in. How much would it take?"

"What makes you think I can be bought?"

Truth be known, life had taught her that almost anyone could be. "Name your price."

"What if it's too high?"

Money was certainly no object. "Try me."

"What if that's my price...*you?*"

Not expecting a solicitation for personal favors, she swallowed her immediate urge to tell him what he could do with himself. Betraying her true reaction wouldn't earn her any Brownie points, and the last thing she needed was to put Kaminsky on the defensive. Then for sure he'd railroad her straight back to the authorities.

But was he serious?

Was this really a come-on?

Inexplicably, a bizarre thrill shot through her, making her belly flutter and her throat tighten. Angela told herself that her physical reaction was one of revulsion added to a healthy dose of fear. And that she sincerely hoped the bounty hunter was merely playing games with her.

For some reason, she couldn't read Micah Kaminsky as easily as she could most men.

Then again, she dealt with professionals on a daily basis. Men who got by on their brains instead of brawn. A logical choice after rejecting her father and everything that reminded her of the old way of life.

The light turned green and he applied his concentration to the traffic that was moving again.

Playing for time, Angela forced herself to say, "Uh, as to your price for helping me…perhaps we could work something out."

Her heart was pounding. Under normal circumstances, she wouldn't even give a man like Kaminsky the time of day. No way would she actually sleep with him. But he didn't have to know that.

"I thought you didn't eye-bat."

"I don't." The tight knot at the back of her throat made it difficult to sound natural. "And you weren't even looking at me, anyway, so how would you know?"

"I've got ears. That was some pretty clear *verbal* eye-batting if I ever heard it."

"So what if it was?" she returned. She quickly reminded him, "I *am* innocent. And I'd do just about anything to keep from going to prison."

"*Just about?*" he repeated.

"I do have standards."

"Nice to know that I meet them."

Not having a ready response, Angela swallowed hard.

This was one game she was no damn good at—making promises for favors, especially sexual ones, that she had no intention of fulfilling. Her style was straightforward. Normally, she shot from the hip and worried about consequences later.

She had to keep in mind that these weren't normal circumstances.

And that going to prison would kill her.

Humiliated once again...her pride shattered...she might as well be dead.

Not having a suicidal bone in her body, however, Angela renewed her determination to finish what she'd started. With no faith in the justice system that had impoverished an innocent wife who'd had three kids to support while her husband served time, no trust in her fellow man except for her mother and siblings, she had no choice but to do whatever was necessary to save herself.

A lesson she'd learned all too young.

The Thunderbird drifted into the left lane, turned west, then sped away from the lake. And Angela suddenly awoke from her self-pitying stupor and realized where they were headed. The Hilton Hotel loomed before them on Michigan Avenue. Surely Kaminsky didn't take her nebulous offer as an agreement...surely he didn't mean to take her directly to the hotel to collect....

Holding her breath, Angela wondered how she was going to get herself out of this fix.

IT TOOK A LOT to leave Angela Dragon tongue-tied— Micah would give her that. Sliding the sunglasses back down to the bridge of his nose, he thanked the gods for the respite, temporary as it might be. He'd put his fatigue at bay to come after her, but his hold on energy was becoming more tenuous each moment he spent in the woman's exhausting company.

She suddenly broke the tranquillity with a belligerent "I didn't agree to anything yet."

Was that a warning tone he caught in her words? "Who said you did?"

"So don't get carried away."

When he realized her attention was focused on the hotel ahead, he almost laughed out loud. He'd merely been trying to get to Angela with the remark about *her* being the price...though the concept had its merits. No question that she was beautiful. Sexy. Spirited. He'd bet she'd be as much of a dragon lady in bed as she was out. She'd never let him get any respite.

Dragonlady.

Though the description fit, he figured she wouldn't see that. What's more, she would probably be furious if she knew what he was thinking.

With knowledge came a grin that he couldn't repress even as they shot across Michigan Avenue and put distance between themselves and the hotel. And he swallowed a grin at her smothered sigh of relief. Angela Dragon might be tough in most situations, but she hadn't learned to protect her vulnerable middle. Now he had her number and, if necessary, would use the knowledge to his advantage.

"You never did give me a straight answer," she said a few blocks later as Union Station came into view.

"About?"

"Whether or not you could be...persuaded...to let me finish what I came for."

Tempted to continue the game, Micah chose to save his trump card. Besides, he needed his wits about him if he meant to get her on that train with a minimum of fuss.

"You'd be wasting your time," he said instead.

"That's not for you to say."

"And you'd get yourself into hot water for sure."

"Not if I'm careful."

He gave her a look. "Like you were at the fashion show?"

"What could Mariscano have done to me with all those people around?"

At the reminder, he checked his mirrors, but as far as he could tell, the coast was clear. "I didn't see anyone trying to stop *me* from hauling you off."

"Put it down to unusual circumstances. People get light-headed about weddings."

"And you don't?"

"God forbid."

She'd mumbled the last, making Micah wonder what she had against weddings, especially since she specialized in them. Maybe being in the business numbed her to the magic. From the privacy of his sunglasses he gave her a thorough once-over. She'd make one hell of a spectacle on her own wedding day, assuming anyone would ever be brave enough—or nuts enough—to take her on. Even disheveled and with her hair all mussed, she made his groin tighten.

"So what about it?" she pressed.

"I have a mission," he finally said, "and you're it."

"You're saying you can't be bribed?"

"Let's say letting you loose wouldn't be in my best interests."

She sank into a black silence, glaring out the side window. He could practically hear her mental wheels turning, but he hadn't a clue what was going on in her head.

Nothing good for him, he was certain.

West of Canal, he pulled in to a Self-Park and prepared for a fight. Man, he didn't need this. He didn't have the heart for it—or the stamina. Energywise, he was running low. What he *did* need was more coffee to stay alert. Mainlining would be a good idea at this point. Truth be told, if only he had a choice, he'd dump Angela Dragon and leave her to her own devices. Maybe she'd earn those cement overshoes.

Even as he thought it, the notion bothered him more than it should.

"How about making a pact?" he suggested as he guided the car into an empty slot. "You come along quietly, and you won't have any more aching body parts or bruises than you do now."

"Is that a threat?"

He sighed. "Call it a prediction."

He could see she was still working on some new scheme—her dark, almond-shaped eyes gave her away.

But she said, "I'm not partial to aches and bruises."

Neither an agreement nor a denial.

Micah figured that was the closest to a promise that he could expect to wring out of her. He left the car and took a careful look around to make certain no one was paying them any mind.

Reassured, he opened the passenger door with a last plea for sanity. "Don't make this any harder on either of us than it has to be."

For whatever it took, he would bring her back to Nevada, even if he had to drag her by the hair, kicking and screaming. Having given his word, he had no choice.

But she seemed relaxed, asking, "What's with the train station instead of the airport?"

He should have known she wouldn't leave it be. They crossed the street, his fingers lightly hooked around her upper arm, his gaze sharp on the surrounding area.

"You have something against riding the rails?"

"It isn't the fastest way anywhere."

"But it *is* safe," he countered.

She arched both eyebrows. "For whom?"

He twinged inside but didn't let it show. "I'm not the one in trouble."

"And no one's chasing me but you."

"Hopefully."

"What do you mean, *hopefully?*" She stopped directly before the station doors while the few midday passengers circled them. "Do you know something you're not telling me?"

"Nothing specific. A gut feeling." One that prompted him to look over his shoulder yet again. "I'd rather err on the side of caution."

"Than what?"

Tempted to gag her already, Micah wondered how he would put up with Angela's company long distance without doing her bodily harm. He swung open the old brass-and-glass door and propelled her through the opening toward the staircase. The station's pale-marble-and-dark-wood lobby was visible below. Suddenly she stopped. He thought she was being stubborn, but at second glance he saw that the damned dress was responsible. The tail end of the gown's train was caught in another door.

What a pain!

Irritated, he glared down its length. "How do you get rid of that thing?"

"Don't even think about it!" Angela warned him. "Getting this gown back to Vida intact is my responsibility." With her free hand, she gathered the material waterfalling behind her. "The door..."

Which was logistically impossible to reach unless he let go of her. "Promise to behave?"

"I always behave."

Angela seemed thoroughly caught up in protecting the dress from further damage. On guard, Micah reluctantly released her arm. She didn't try a thing...until he moved back to the entrance, hunched over, one hand on the door, the other arm extended, reaching...

Then she bolted, yanking hard. The train popped free with a spray of pearls and crystals rolling across the smooth floor. Micah grabbed at the fluttering material, but it sailed right through his fingers. And when he lunged to his feet to go after her, he slipped and slid as if he were trying to run on ball bearings. He landed on one knee even as Angela flew straight down the stairs.

Back on his feet, Micah rushed to the rail, quickly assessing the situation below. Only a few people noticed the runaway bride. A couple of boys in blue, whose backs were to them, headed for the commuter waiting rooms. If Angela caught their attention, asked the cops for help, what then? She wouldn't do it, he assured himself grimly, racing down the stairs after her. That wouldn't help her get what she wanted—other than being rid of him.

But if Angela lied about her identity, got the cops to believe he was stalking her, chances were he'd be behind bars within the hour.

Having vowed never to become personally acquainted with another jail cell, Micah found good use for the adrenaline pumping through him. He intercepted Angela at the bottom of the stairs. She tried to dodge him, but he caught her by the waist and spun her around, then pulled her body tight to his for an intimate face-to-face. A low sound of frustration flew from her lips and he thought she was opening her mouth to scream.

For a foolish second, he thought to kiss her quiet....

All traces of good humor having fled at the sight of the cops, however, Micah couldn't work up any enthusiasm for the notion.

He grimly said, "If I were you, I'd think very carefully about my next move."

Angela's mouth snapped shut. She was heaving for breath, her full breasts pulsing against his chest, a situation troubling Micah despite his good sense. Heat rose in an uncomfortable direction, a fact he attempted to ignore.

He set the sunglasses atop his head so she could see he was deadly serious when he said, "You're going back to Nevada. We can do this the easy way or the hard way. I was hoping for easy."

"We don't always get what we want."

A brief glimpse past the assured exterior tugged at him. Something in her eyes...

Damn it all!

So maybe she was innocent. *Probably* was innocent. That wasn't for him to worry about. He had a simple assignment: get the lady back where she belonged. Leave her to the justice system.

Smothering a sudden surge of empathy the latter thought caused him, he said, "Let's go."

His fingers fastening like a manacle around her wrist, Micah turned her toward the ticket counter at the same moment that he heard the *ping* of a silenced bullet striking the rail between them.

Chapter Three

Torn between fighting and screaming for help in spite of spotting a couple of cops, Angela reeled when Kaminsky used his leverage on her wrist to whip her around 180 degrees. He started dragging her back up the stairs so rapidly that the awkward weight and bulk of the wedding gown nearly tripped her.

"What do you think you're doing?" she demanded, battling the material.

"Trying to keep you alive!"

About to demand further explanation, she was startled into silence by a soft pop to her right. The unfamiliar sound brought the fine hairs along her arms to attention...her imagination connecting the echo to a bullet inscribed with her name.

"Kaminsky, what in the—?"

"*Not now!*" Propelling her in front of him, he shoved at her backside to keep the momentum going.

And her finely honed instincts for self-preservation kept her from arguing. Questions could wait. Heart pounding, Angela lifted her skirts with both hands and scrambled up the staircase faster than she'd descended.

Even so, she chanced a peek over her shoulder.

Below, staring in their direction, a man in a broad-brimmed hat and sunglasses casually rose from a high-backed wooden bench. An open newspaper half-hid his lower body.

And a gun equipped with a silencer?

Her adrenaline pumping, Angela fled to the upper landing and burst through the door to the street, where her nemesis once more grabbed her by the arm. As if she needed encouragement to keep moving! When she came to an unexpected halt because the door again slammed on the damned train—this time through no fault of her own—she nearly shrieked in frustration.

"That's it!" Kaminsky griped.

Without ceremony, he seized the fabric directly behind her bottom and yanked. She winced at the tearing sound and silently vowed to make this up to Vida. After all, how important was a ruined wedding gown when compared with a possible trip to the morgue?

Free of the encumbrance, she moved with much less effort as they raced into the street, dodging cars as they crossed. A parking lot had never seemed so welcome.

Another glance back assured Angela the ruined train was proving to be multipurpose—a somewhat odd blessing in disguise. In coming after them, the suspicious-looking man had exited the same door. His mistake. His feet tangling in the discarded yardage sent him into a crazy dance, and he unsuccessfully fought for balance.

Down he went.

"Yes!" Angela shouted breathlessly.

Up came his arm, a wicked-looking gun clutched in his hand.

Not needing to see more, she sprinted past Kaminsky, forcing him to pick up speed to stay even with her. If more bullets whizzed by them, she hadn't a clue, since the blood rushing through her head was far too loud.

The afternoon sun glinting off its midnight blue finish, the Thunderbird appeared larger than life, a beacon of safety.

This time when the bounty hunter opened the passenger door, she voluntarily jumped in and rubbernecked for a view through the rear window. Gasping for breath, she observed the would-be assassin approach the street and wave.

A black limousine crept forward and slid to a stop at the curb beside him.

A series of beeps and the engine starting seemingly on its own astonished Angela from her watch. Kaminsky was opening the driver's door. He jumped inside and threw the car into Reverse practically before he settled behind the wheel.

"Do you have a thing for gadgets in general or only the ones you can load on your car?"

She was still trying to catch her breath. Silence his only answer, he shifted and the coupe jumped forward, her heart rate zooming with it.

"In case you didn't notice," she informed him, now craning out the side window, "the bastard's not alone in the car."

"I noticed."

The villains had the edge—their vehicle was circling the parking lot, heading for the only exit. It didn't take a genius to realize the limo would cut off their escape route.

"What are we going to do now?" she asked.

He slammed on the brakes. She flew forward, catching the sun-crisped dash with both hands.

"Seat belt!"

As he threw the car in Reverse and backed down the aisle at a dizzying speed, Angela followed the grimly issued order. A cloud of doom threatened to smother her. If the man with the gun didn't finish her off, this driving might.

"Did I tell you I get carsick?"

"Open the window before you throw up."

"Nice, Kaminsky," she muttered. "Did you learn that in Sensitivity 101?"

At the end of the aisle he shifted direction so fast that Angela doubted the car came to a full stop in between. And she was certain they lurched around the corner on only two wheels. Her stomach roiled. She swallowed hard and strained for sight of the limo.

"It's gone!"

"Not exactly." He sounded even more grim. "How do you feel about a little game of chicken?"

Turning in her seat, she gaped. From the other end of the lot, the limo was heading straight at them and they weren't slowing down.

"Are you crazy?"

"My legacy from Insanity 102," he agreed, his foot pressing the accelerator, the engine revving with a grumbling roar.

Angela's life flashed before her eyes. Like a dark avenging angel, the limo was bearing down on them. She briefly contemplated jumping from the moving vehicle, but that would undoubtedly seal the lid on her coffin.

"Hang on, Dragonlady!"

Holding her breath, she white-knuckled the dash and prayed.

Before them, the limousine braked and bucked at the same time Kaminsky muscled the car into a right turn. Ahead, at the other end of the aisle, a half space gaped between two cars parked on the outside perimeter of the unfenced lot. Behind them, the limo was already following.

And inside herself, she was trying not to panic, though her sense of doom was multiplying in scary proportions.

Mesmerized by the abbreviated opening that seemed far too tight for even a smaller vehicle, she was certain he meant to plow right through.

"Anything you want to get off your conscience before you meet your Maker?" she asked him.

"No. How about you?"

He barely slowed down.

Angela sucked in her breath, as if doing so would magically shrink the Thunderbird. Her mental sorcery worked—they managed to shoot through the gap without so much as a scrape of metal on metal. They charged out of the lot, over the sidewalk and straight off the high curb. When the wheels slammed into the pavement with a clatter of worn metal parts, Angela's head snapped back and her teeth nicked the side of her cheek.

Blood pooled in her mouth, the bitter taste and the sting of raw flesh assuring her she was still alive.

A bit of fancy maneuvering on Kaminsky's part avoided a collision with several moving vehicles. Around them, brakes screeched and horns blared in protest. If he noticed, Kaminsky didn't seem the least unnerved. He kept going. Within seconds they were cruising right along with the westbound traffic.

Breathing more easily, she checked on the villains' progress. As its driver attempted to follow their lead, the limo crunched into one of the parked cars and stopped dead.

"Game point," she murmured.

"At least for the moment."

Not about to comment on his pessimism, Angela let

go of the dash and sank back into her squeaky seat, her body feeling as though she'd run a four-minute mile. Her abductor, on the other hand, appeared as cool as a cucumber...right in his element. Could be he'd done some time driving race cars. Or taxis. In her opinion, being a passenger in either could prove to be an equally risky business.

"So, how long have you had a death wish?"

"You're alive, aren't you?"

Angela couldn't argue with that. But her adrenaline was pumping. Her thoughts were congealing. And she was beginning to wonder...

"Who was that guy after, anyway? Me? Or you?"

"*I* haven't made any enemies lately."

"Meaning you have at some time or other." Maybe she had made a mistake as to the assassin's intentions. She seized on the possibility. "Then he could be someone from *your* past. An old bounty you turned in come back to get revenge."

"If you believe that, you're fooling yourself."

His matter-of-fact tone discouraged debate, and yet she couldn't let it go. "But why would anyone want me dead?"

"Gosh, I don't know." He didn't try to hide the bite in his words. "Let's think about that. It couldn't have to do with your subtlety."

Realizing she'd had similar thoughts while being hauled out of the exposition center, she asked, "You think someone like Joey Mariscano would order a hit because I interrupted his date with his daughter?"

"Unless it's someone else you annoyed by getting on his nerves with your incessant arguments."

His pointed expression rankled.

"I'd say you have that one locked, Kaminsky. If you

hadn't come along and grabbed me out of that fashion show—''

"You might be dead now."

Unwilling to admit the bounty hunter might have saved her neck, Angela stayed on the attack.

"You're the one who insisted the train would be safer than a plane. Why is that? If you're so hot to get me back to Las Vegas to claim the reward on my head, I would think you'd want to move fast."

His "I was trying to throw them off the scent" didn't convince her.

"Throw who? Mariscano's thugs? How would you have known about them? How could you have guessed what I was going to do ahead of time? And how did anyone figure I'd skipped the state in the first place?"

"You were being watched."

"By whom?"

To her frustration, he went tight-lipped.

Meaning to pursue that line of questioning, she was distracted by his edging the car into the right lane that led directly onto the expressway. Could he be heading for the airport, after all?

Her immediate fate uppermost in her mind, she asked, "And what do you plan to do now?"

"Drive."

They zoomed down the ramp faster than necessary and zipped across two lanes.

"Where to? The airport? Another train station? The garbage dump?" When he didn't say, the worst-case scenario popped into her mind. "Not across country!"

As if being indicted and shot at weren't bad enough. The thought of spending two or three days in this man's company horrified her.

"If so, we're heading north," she informed him, trying to keep her blood pressure from rising. "The *wrong* direction."

"Exactly."

Angela told herself to stay calm, but it was nearly impossible. With a single word he'd confirmed her worst nightmare. Her life was spinning out of her control, and she couldn't seem to do a damn thing about it. The last time she'd felt so helpless had been the day her father had been incarcerated....

She'd been a teenager then, Angela reminded herself. Hardly more than a kid. The experience had been traumatic, but it had built character. She was proud of the woman she'd become. And she was perfectly capable of taking back her life. Now that she could do so calmly, she quickly assessed her situation.

Rather than trying to get answers out of the uncooperative bounty hunter, she needed to concentrate on using him...then losing him.

"Mariscano's place is north," she stated as they passed the split that would take them out to the airport.

"So?"

Wondering if he was thinking on like lines, she said, "So, if we get inside, maybe we can find something to prove that he set me up."

"That's not my concern."

"Well, it's *mine*. That's why I came halfway across the country, as you well know. And *that*, by the way, is why you have a job to do in the first place. Because of *me*. You'll make a good buck on my head...therefore, the least you owe me is some consideration."

He glanced her way. Despite the sunglasses, she read his amazement.

"Logic 103?"

"Much more advanced," she responded, praying

she'd gotten through to him. "And what could stopping for a teensy while hurt?"

"You, for one, maybe permanently. And if I'm *really* lucky...*me*."

"Is that whining I hear?" Taunting him might not be smart, but she couldn't help herself. "Is the big strong bounty hunter afraid of anyone who's not half his size?"

"You're a hell of a lot bigger than half my size."

As if he were afraid of her! Besides, he knew she meant Mariscano's goons. "You're avoiding."

"Psychology—"

She cut him off. "Personal therapist."

"You see a shrink and you're still this messed up?"

That did it. How did he get off criticizing her personally? He didn't have the first idea of who she really was.

"Messed up how?" she demanded. "Because I want to prove my innocence? Because I have the guts to try without involving anyone else?"

"You've already involved me."

"Your choice, not mine," she reminded him. "I didn't throw *you* over my shoulder and drag you out of the exposition center. As for what went on at the train station...you didn't act out of the goodness of your heart. You were protecting your own butt *and* your investment." On a roll, she picked up speed. "The authorities don't want me returned dead. At least, I assume I haven't made a Post Office wall yet. Something happens to me, and you'll have a lot of explaining to do. Get me back safe and you'll trade me for a nice monetary reward."

He had the audacity to appear aggravated when he demanded, "Are you done?"

"Not quite." Unable to help herself, she tried appealing to his sense of fair play. "I have a much bigger stake in this than you do. If I can get the goods on Mariscano, *my* reward will be keeping my freedom...and my good name."

Silent for a moment, he finally asked, "Is a good name so important that you had to change yours?"

Her argument obviously having gone for naught, Angela ground her teeth in frustration. So he knew about her father. Why should she be surprised? There was a time when Tomas Dragonetti had been infamous. And reporters had long noses. They smelled the old, faded trail of a story and dug up all the dirt they could from the past. Every nuance of the relationship between her and her father had undoubtedly been laid bare by every newspaper in the country. Kaminsky probably knew almost as much about her as she did herself.

Unable to keep her personal bitterness at bay, she said, "I didn't know men in your profession read."

"I skim the headlines while searching for the comic strips."

Tit for tat.

She didn't seem to be able to get a thing out of the man except sarcasm. Not that giving up was in her nature. Her mind was still racing, looking for some out, some way to delay the inevitable and finish what she'd started. They were nearing the city limits. She didn't have much time. Once he'd gone far enough, he'd never turn back. Knowing that wresting the wheel from his hands wouldn't be smart—whether or not it was actually possible—she hoped changing her tune might sway him.

"Look, you don't have to step one foot into Mariscano's house," she promised amiably. "You don't have to do a thing but make a little detour so that *I* can. Then I'll go with you willingly."

"You're deluded. He won't throw his doors open

wide for you—at least, not so you can play Private Eye."

"He won't be there yet. And he won't expect *me* to be." Thinking of the friendly housekeeper, Angela said, "I bet I can talk myself in."

All she'd have to do was figure out some story relating to the wedding gown she was temporarily trapped in. Like...she was helping Mariscano surprise his little DeeDee with this fabulous design. If the housekeeper didn't look too closely at the raggedy rear of the dress or at her disheveled hair, the story just might work.

Before she could try to convince him, Kaminsky surprised her by asking, "So what if you manage to get inside the house—then what?"

Her pulse surged with renewed hope. "Then I search his office."

"Makes sense. Probably has a written confession laid out for you, too—signed and nicely tied up with a blue ribbon."

"Or a red one," she suggested caustically, her spirits plunging once more. "Get over yourself, Kaminsky. I'm not a ditz, as you keep suggesting. Not knowing what I'm looking for doesn't make me stupid. Haven't you ever heard the expression 'I can't tell you what I want, but when I see it, I'll know'?" At least, she thought that's how it went. "Well, I will."

"You're convinced you're going to find something incriminating."

"Given the opportunity," she bluffed, knowing perfectly well that she could be on a wild-goose chase. That Mariscano could be innocent...at least, of setting her up. After their little face-to-face, though, her gut instincts told her she was right on the money. "So what about it?"

The bounty hunter chose that moment to clam up. Again. Angela wanted to scream in frustration. What was with him? Anxious to figure another angle she could use to snow him, she almost missed the fact that he abandoned the expressway at the exit nearest Joey Mariscano's home turf.

HE WAS GOING TO REGRET this, Micah groused to himself. He was convinced of it. So why didn't he keep on driving straight out of the state? Maybe because Angela had made a case about trying to prove her own innocence without involving anyone else. He had to respect that.

Or maybe he was a sucker for hollow cheeks and almond-shaped eyes, especially when they glittered with excitement, as they'd done when she was on a roll.

Noting she was trying to neaten her hair as they cut through the suburb, he said, "You realize we won't have a lot of time to get in and out. He could come back any moment."

He wasn't going to hang around long enough to have to explain himself to anyone. Not to Mariscano. Certainly not to the cops.

"I'll take what I can get."

He didn't believe her, of course. She'd say whatever she had to so that he'd do what she wanted. He was an idiot for caving in.

Several minutes later, turning onto the tree-lined street off Sheridan Road for the second time that day, he wondered if Mariscano's society neighbors knew what he actually did to be able to afford one of these mansions. Then again, maybe they didn't care. To some, business was business and money was money—didn't much matter the source as long as you made enough of the green stuff. Besides, who said his neighbors walked a straight path?

And speaking of neighbors...

As he pulled up in front of the house, he noticed the elderly woman next door was still in her yard. Though she wore a big straw hat and heavy cotton gloves and clutched a pruner to her sagging breast, her attention was already fixed on them rather than on her flowers.

"Aren't you going to pull in the driveway?" she asked.

"So we can be cut off from the street if we need to make a quick getaway?"

"True. And I guess a woman flouncing around in a bridal gown wouldn't bring unwanted attention to us." She didn't bother to hide her sarcasm. "Or a car that's seen better days."

Why had he bothered to resist? She would peck at him like a chicken at its feed until there was nothing left.

Normally he would remain impervious, but a man without sleep was weak, Micah decided, moving the car. Besides, he grudgingly admitted, she had a point about being obvious. Despite its powerful V-8 engine, not even the teenagers in the swank neighborhood would be caught driving a car that was nearly ten years old and starting to rust around the edges.

He pulled all the way through the driveway and around the back of the contemporary villa, out of sight of the street.

They alighted simultaneously.

Angela's eyes widened. "I thought you were going to wait for me here."

He raised an eyebrow at her ingenuous expression. He'd undoubtedly wait until the cows came home, for she sounded as if she *wanted* him out of her hair for a while. Time enough to hatch an escape plan?

"I never said I'd stay in the car," he noted.

"But I don't want to involve you."

"You aren't."

Her features smoothed as she accepted his insistence and led the way to the side door. He could almost hear the wheels in her head turning and meshing as she tried to figure out a way to dump him. When no one answered the bell, her mouth pulled into a tight line. Not that she gave up so easily. But after ringing and knocking for several minutes to no avail, she appeared ready to explode.

Or was it to cry in frustration?

"Can you believe the luck? The housekeeper's gone! And we can't even jimmy a window or anything. Not with this!" Indicating the entry pad that was part of the security system, she looked as if she'd like to punch it.

He was surprised the property wasn't fenced and gated, but he suspected the local chamber of commerce had a say in that. Probably wanted to promote the innate safety of the suburb as a feature.

"You expected less?" he asked.

"I expected to get inside."

Feeling the short hairs on the back of his neck rise, Micah turned to see the nosy neighbor peering at them through parted foliage where bushes separated the properties.

"I'll cut you a deal," he said. "You go distract the busybody—" he crooked his head toward the elderly woman "—and I'll see what I can do."

"Can you work a miracle?"

"Doubtful. But this system doesn't look too complicated."

Especially since he was familiar with the manufacturer and the model and was competent at whatever he put his hand to. But to Micah's knowledge, breaking and entering hadn't yet been legalized—not even if the victim was a big-time criminal—and the last thing he needed was a witness.

"Go on." He pushed Angela toward the bushes. "I'll check for a way in. Keep the old lady's attention on you until I signal."

Micah hoped he wasn't being foolish letting her get so far away from him. First, she was the one who was desperate to get inside the house. Plus, where would she go? As she'd said, she wasn't exactly inconspicuous in a bridal gown. And this wasn't the city. Posh suburbs weren't known for their great public transportation systems—everyone had a Mercedes or a Jag, if not a chauffeured limo.

The limo thought reminded him of the hired gun in the train station. He hadn't examined the situation too closely before, but now he wondered how the bastard had known not only where to wait, but when.

Realizing Angela had stopped and was staring at him suspiciously, he asked, "Do we have a deal, or what? Go create a diversion."

With a last glance over her shoulder at him, she did as he urged and sauntered toward the curious neighbor.

All senses on alert to possible trouble, Micah strolled to his car and opened the trunk.

Chapter Four

Angela wondered what Kaminsky thought he could do with a security system, then decided he might have had some experience with them tracking down criminals on the run.

Criminal on the run.

That's what she would be if she didn't find something to prove otherwise. And she couldn't find anything if she couldn't get into the house. Wondering what Micah was pulling from his trunk, she called out to the neighbor.

"Good afternoon." The bushes suddenly shook and the opening disappeared, but Angela persisted. "Can you help me?"

The branches parted, as if by magic. A wizened face peeked at her from the other side.

"I saw you earlier," the woman stated, her voice surprisingly strong despite her frail appearance. "But you were wearing regular clothes. You marry that fellah there?"

Aghast at the prospect, she tried not to sound offended. "As a matter of fact, no."

Realizing the neighbor was squinting over her shoulder—most likely trying to get a glimpse of Kaminsky—

she shifted to block the view. She, too, was wondering what he was up to, but keeping the woman's attention was in both of their best interests. They didn't need a busybody calling in the local police.

In an attempt to distract the elderly woman, Angela asked, "Do you know what time DeeDee planned to come home?" She tried to sound as if they were girlfriends.

The old lady inspected her bridal gown up, down and sideways. "You must have married *someone*," she stated, as if she hadn't heard Angela's question.

"Not yet, actually."

"Ah, the wedding hasn't taken place, then." Her wrinkled face brightened. "Is it to be here?"

Caught without a comeback, Angela mumbled, "Uh, no-o-o—"

"You need flowers. Some to carry." Her face alight now, her faded eyes glowing, the neighbor said, "And some for your hair." Waving her pruning shears, she asked, "What are your favorites?"

Angela was touched by the woman's unexpected generosity. "Thank you, but everything's taken care of."

"You're sure?" The sparkle in the old eyes dimmed and the thin mouth trembled.

Angela couldn't bear her disappointment. "Except for my hair. Since I don't have a veil, I *could* use a flower to put in my hair." A big one that would hide the bald patch, she thought wryly. "You pick."

"Any special color?"

"Something vibrant."

The old lady nodded and toddled away, the long skirts of her old-fashioned gardening dress flowing around her.

Her tongue worrying the raw spot inside her mouth, Angela took a quick glance around. No sign of the bounty hunter. She only hoped he didn't set off the security system's alarm. Then they'd both be in hot water.

"Here you go," the neighbor said, holding out a stem with dozens of tiny red blooms. "Salvia. One of my favorites."

"How lovely." Smiling, she secured the flower in what was left of her upswept hairdo. "Thank you."

"You're the one who's lovely, child. Any time you want some fresh flowers, you come see Miriam."

Realizing the neighborhood snoop was in reality a lonely senior citizen, she was as truthful as she could be. "If I had the chance, I would love to—"

A sharp whistle cut her off.

Kaminsky?

Assuming the whistle was the purported signal, Angela glanced back toward the limestone building. She couldn't spot the bounty hunter anywhere. Hopefully, because he'd gotten inside. Her excitement surged.

"I'm sorry, but I really have to go now."

"You tell your young man to be more respectful than to expect you to come to some crude summons," Miriam advised her. "You whistle for your pet, not the woman you love. Make him appreciate you from your first day together."

The first and the last, Angela hoped.

Impulsively hugging the frail woman, she shot away as a second, more impatient-sounding whistle demanded her attention. She rounded the rear of the house only to come upon open French doors. No movement in the room beyond. Fearing some kind of trap, she hesitated before entering.

Heart pounding, she anxiously called, "Kaminsky?"

"What's taking you so long?"

Though she could hear him clearly, he remained out of sight.

Her suspicion unappeased—what if one of Mariscano's men had caught him?—she asked, "Where are you?"

"Inside. Where I thought *you* wanted to be."

The caustic reply eased her mind.

Swallowing hard, she admitted what was really bothering her—compounding her flight from Nevada with another crime. Regardless, she stepped into the dining room, bunching her full skirts so they wouldn't brush against anything breakable. Her pulse skittered as she took in the room, recognizing the crook's touch everywhere. Undoubtedly he'd paid an interior designer to choose the basics, but collectibles in excess covered the walls and every available surface, even as his gold rings covered his fingers.

More Is Better seemed to be Joey Mariscano's motto in his personal life in addition to his professional one.

That thought reminded her of their immediate purpose. "Where are you? We need to find the office."

But the bounty hunter was a few steps ahead of her. "The hallway," he called, his deep-timbred voice echoing her way. "And I think I've found it."

Angela rushed across the dining room to join him. On the opposite end of the hall, he was opening a door.

"This is it," he announced.

Propped against the doorjamb, he scanned the room. Eager to find her proof, Angela hurried past him, her arm brushing his, then sensed his shift in attention. She turned. He was staring openly. Without the shield of his sunglasses, his blue eyes pierced her. Made her feel itchy all over.

Vulnerable.

She frowned. "What?"

"The flower—"

"Miriam, the neighbor—"

"—suits you."

Caught unawares by the unexpected compliment, Angela found herself speechless, unsure how to respond to this man in a noncombative mode.

And the way he was savoring her with his eyes reminded her that he was, indeed, a man. With his sharp Eastern European features and rugged build, a far more attractive one than she'd cared to admit earlier.

Skin sizzling at the silent concession, she dropped her gaze and noticed what he'd fetched from the trunk of the Thunderbird—he was wearing a vest with multiple pockets, several of which bulged. What secrets could they be hiding? With that question in mind, she gazed up at him...

Only to find him staring even more intently.

Which flustered her into action.

Determined to appear cool and unaffected, she casually moved to the center of the room that reeked of Italian leather and lemon polish. To negate his effect on her, she purposefully took inventory.

Two couches, a chair and ottoman were grouped around an oversize fireplace. The walls on either side were lined with book-filled, floor-to-ceiling shelves. At the opposite end of the room, massive mahogany file cabinets flanked an equally massive desk. A kilim carpet shrouded most of the intricate parquet flooring, and several oversize sculptures—including one that belonged in a garden fountain—balanced on pedestals around the room.

"Where to begin?" she murmured, wondering if the

sculpture of the nude woman near the desk was privy to any of the crook's secrets.

"You take the files," Kaminsky suggested. "I'll check the bookshelves. Let's make this quick and get out while the going's good."

Angela nodded. They didn't have time to waste.

She attacked the first file cabinet with the zeal of the self-righteous. Folders revealed Mariscano to be organized and meticulous. Everything in order. No references to her or Here Comes the Bride, of course. As a matter of fact, nothing she found made the Chicago businessman appear anything but legitimate. She only hoped that she hadn't gone on a wild-goose chase, after all.

Not that she'd assumed getting her hands on information that could clear her would be easy, Angela reminded herself.

"Find anything?" she asked, turning toward Kaminsky.

"Other than law books? How about a false front hiding a notebook computer and portable printer?"

Catching sight of the equipment Mariscano had taken care to hide, she widened her eyes. *Eureka!* "Why didn't you say something?" No slouch with a computer herself, she started across the room.

Hunched over the keyboard, Kaminsky paid her no mind. His fingers were flying along the keys. *Such large hands to be so dexterous.* When she got a glimpse of the screen, she noted he was already into the main directory.

The realization stopped Angela dead in her tracks. Her exhilaration waned.

"You're wasting your time. Mariscano wouldn't store any significant information in a computer without securing the system with a code."

"He did."

Which hadn't stopped Kaminsky...

"Let's just take the thing with us," she said, her emotions seesawing. "It *is* portable."

His expression disbelieving, he said, "You're the one with the death wish. You think Mariscano would let anyone abscond with all his private records and not do something about it? We leave the place as we found it—with no trace that we've ever been here."

Angela's mouth went dry. She let other questions go unasked. For now. Better that he finesse the computer than take precious time to explain how he'd broken in to it.

Or how he'd breached the house's security system in the first place...

Going back to her search, she again wondered about the secrets in Kaminsky's vest pockets.

The folders in the second cabinet proved as unrevealing as those in the first. Finished scanning them a quarter of an hour later, she cursed her luck. In frustration, she slammed the bottom drawer.

"Nothing."

And looked to the bounty hunter, hoping for better news.

He met her gaze. "Nothing here yet, either. At least, I haven't found anything to do with you."

Thinking it wouldn't be a bad idea to have whatever information she could hold over Mariscano's head as insurance, she figured Kaminsky wouldn't go for it. He was too worried about his precious neck to stretch it out any more than he already had.

"It's the desk, then," she muttered.

"What if it's not? What if we both strike out?"

Even suspecting Mariscano wouldn't keep anything to

do with *business* elsewhere in the house, she said, "We have plenty of rooms to search."

He glanced at his watch. "Only, we don't have plenty of time. Someone's bound to come home soon. I'd better finish up here."

Rather than argue, Angela sat in the leather chair behind the desk and took inventory until she spotted the day-by-day calendar.

Mariscano's schedule! Why hadn't she thought to check it out before?

"I may have something here," she said, flipping to the date when this mess had started.

Kaminsky glanced her way. "And I'm printing a file that might prove useful. Mariscano seems to have organized his operations by city—there's a file labeled LV—"

"Las Vegas!"

"Right. A printout we can take with us."

"Good," she said, turning back to what she hoped would be a gold mine.

She paged to the date they'd had the meeting in her office. Opposite 10:00 a.m. he'd penciled in "L.V.—A.D." L.V. again for Las Vegas, A.D. for Angela Dragon. The only other notation on that page was for 9:00 p.m. "W., Mir." Not too helpful. Scanning similar abbreviated entries on succeeding pages didn't yield the clue she was hoping for. Her initials never appeared again, and she would need a decoder ring to sort out Mariscano's encryptions.

Hopefully, the computer printout would yield something more enlightening. *If* she'd been correct about knowing what she wanted when she saw it...

Kaminsky had already closed down the computer and replaced the false front. The shelves looked perfectly natural, even though Angela knew what was hidden and where. Stuffing the printout into one of his vest's many pockets, the bounty hunter crossed the room to her.

Not wanting to leave any corner unsearched, she quickly started on the desk drawers, beginning with the middle. Nothing. The drawers on the left were equally unrevealing.

"We need to get out of here," Kaminsky said, even as he crouched beside her. "Just one minute…" He began prodding and poking beneath the desk.

"What are you doing?"

His arm brushed her leg, and even through the material spread gooseflesh up her limb at an alarming rate. Angela was appalled, considering the seriousness of her purpose, that she could so easily be distracted. She rolled her chair to the right, placing some distance between them.

"What are you looking for?" she asked again.

"Springs or pieces that shift. Hidden compartments."

"You do have a love affair with gadgets, don't you?"

"I *appreciate* gadgets." He glanced up at her. "I save my love affairs for women."

His penetrating gaze reminded her of the price he expected her to pay for his help. Breath caught in her throat, she covered her sudden jitters by opening the top drawer on the right and blindly staring in. Suddenly a small leather-bound book came into focus.

"This could be it." Pulling it out, she rose. "Phone numbers."

She had barely opened to the first page before the sound of an engine intruded on the quiet.

Kaminsky flew to his feet. "Our time just ran out."

Pulse racing anew, Angela stepped toward the window and cautiously peered out, remaining far enough back that she wouldn't be seen. Kaminsky stood directly behind her, his proximity making her edgy.

His lips were far too close to her ear when he murmured, "A limo."

Her hair fluttered along her cheek, diverting her until one of the vehicle's doors flew open and a piqued-looking DeeDee stepped out.

"The real bride-to-be." She didn't need to see the father. Backing off, she whispered, "What do we do now?"

"Get the hell out of here."

Pulling her by the arm, he started for the doorway, pausing before the drawer she'd left open. Then he tried to take the leather-bound book from her.

She glared at him and hung on with both hands. "Oh, no, you don't!"

"He'll know someone broke in."

"Maybe he'll assume he left this somewhere else. Who knows when he'll even need to look up a phone number again?" She wrested the book from his grasp. "Either I take the time to look through it now or it's coming with us," she said, knowing the second option was the only realistic one.

"Put the damn book back where you found it!" he ordered.

Quickly sizing up the situation, she figured Kaminsky was too fatigued to really force the issue. His face appeared more drawn than it had earlier. And he looked smaller somehow, as if his body were caving in on him.

As voices raised in argument penetrated the walls, she said, "I'm not leaving it behind. I came for proof that Mariscano set me up, and this is my last hope."

"All right," he finally conceded, even sounding frayed. He shut the open drawer and quickly scanned the room as if checking for anything out of place. "Have it your way, but let's get the hell out of here before we're trapped inside."

Starting to follow him, Angela paused for a second to free her skirts when the material caught on the desk. The yardage bunched in one hand, she closed the door behind her with the other.

Mariscano and his daughter were arguing directly outside the front door.

Stomach knotting with the fear of exposure, she rushed down the hall and through the dining room. As she flew outside, Kaminsky was already easing the French doors closed. He began punching numbers on the keypad.

"The code's not responding," came DeeDee's shrill voice from the driveway side of the house.

"So you hit a wrong number." Her previously doting father sounded exasperated. "Do it again."

Kaminsky finished resetting the alarm and took off, Angela on his heels. And not a moment to spare.

Only when she confronted the Thunderbird parked along the bushes did she wonder if they could possibly get off the property without being seen.

HAVING HAD ENOUGH of his daughter's unrelenting tantrum, Joey Mariscano headed for the solace of his office.

Nearby, a car started. Out of habit he tried to place the engine, but didn't recognize it. Probably some souped-up deal that belonged to a friend of the neighbor's kid.

Entering his office, he slipped out of his jacket and loosened his tie.

What a day!

He'd like to wring Angela Dragon's neck for ruining

it. She'd set DeeDee off, all right, and he hadn't been able to recapture the camaraderie they'd been enjoying. Normally his youngest kid was a pain in the butt—his fault, he supposed, since he'd spoiled her—but for a short while she'd been sweet and all smiles, reminding him of her mother, God bless her soul. As much as he loved DeeDee, he'd be glad to see her married and some other man's headache.

He had enough headaches of his own.

The biggest of which was proving to be a migraine named Angela Dragon.

Outside, the running vehicle moved off, followed by faint crunching noises and a screech. Then all went quiet.

Uncertain how to handle the repercussions of the Dragon situation, he sat behind his desk and let the leather that was as soft as a baby's bottom envelop him. He was always able to think better ensconced in his favorite chair.

His mind whirled with the possibilities. Before he could make any decision, he needed to know what was what.

He shifted in his chair to reach for the telephone and thrust his leg forward under the desk. The leather sole of his shoe slipped and he felt something underfoot. Reaching down to retrieve the object, he figured he was going to have to speak to the new housekeeper. Again. One more time and she was out. He didn't tolerate sloppy work in any of his operations, and especially not in his home.

Straightening, he frowned when he saw what he'd retrieved.

What was a pearl doing on his office floor?

MICAH KEPT WATCH for a tail as they headed away from the scene of the crime as fast as he dared—the last thing he needed was to be pulled over for speeding, and after he'd gotten them away from Mariscano's place without being shot at again.

They'd gotten off lucky. He'd figured the T-bird's engine would alert the household. And when he'd squeezed through a tight opening in the bushes, he'd been certain they'd be able to hear Angela complaining—despite her trying to take charge, he'd taken off across the neighbor's property. No one had seemed to notice.

Heading onto the expressway, he told an amazingly silent Angela, "Looks like we're in the clear."

"Uh-huh."

Micah split his attention between the traffic and what she was doing. Her head was bent, her almond eyes glued to Mariscano's little black book. Her forefinger traced the page, while her lips followed along silently. She frowned. Shook her head. Went on.

"Can't that wait?" he asked.

"Until when?"

"Later."

"Why?" She tore her gaze from the pages. "You have something you want me to do?"

"Two sets of eyes are better than one."

"You said we're in the clear. Are you sure you're not looking for company?"

His response was automatic. "If I wanted company, I'd know where to find it." She encouraged sarcasm.

Truth be told, he wanted her company. Needed it. A constant debate would make it impossible to fall asleep at the wheel. The stop-and-go rush-hour traffic was nearly hypnotizing, and he was having trouble keeping his attention focused on the road ahead. His limbs felt heavy. And he longed for a bed. Any bed. A patch of grass in the shade would do.

"Did you ever take geography in school?" she asked suddenly.

"Why?"

"I just wondered if you had the foggiest notion of where certain states were in relationship to one another. Like Nevada to Illinois, for instance. Nevada *is* southwest of here."

"All of a sudden you're in a hurry to get back? Find what you were looking for in that black book?"

"If it's there, I haven't deciphered it yet. Mariscano has his own shorthand."

"Then what's the rush?"

"I don't exactly look forward to spending more time than I have to in your company."

He should have known she'd take another shot at him. "Nice thanks a man gets for going out of his way."

She gestured toward the sea of cars before them. "*This* is out of the way?"

"*This* is going to confuse anyone who's looking for us. Who would think we'd take a northern route?"

"Us?" she echoed.

"Right." Bullets were indiscriminate. And witnesses inconvenient.

"As in either one of us," she went on doggedly, "or the two of us together?"

"Whatever."

He could feel her frustration, a building wave of energy. That was it. That's what he needed to keep him going. Even as his brain came fully awake, he yawned.

"Sleepy, huh?"

"Tired," he admitted. "Late night." Let her make of that what she would.

"I can drive."

"I'll bet you can."

Only, he couldn't even guess where she'd take him if he fell asleep. Maybe she'd open the passenger door and push...*if* she could figure out how to unlock it.

Angela sighed. "After all we've been through, you don't trust me."

"Should I?" he asked, snorting at her hurt tone. He wondered if acting came naturally to her or if she'd taken lessons.

Traffic had loosened up somewhat. And they were out of the greater metropolitan area. Buildings on either side of the road had become scarce.

"So what's our route?" Angela asked. "We're heading for Wisconsin, right?"

"You do know your geography." He didn't figure telling her would hurt anything. "We'll go through Minnesota, South Dakota, Wyoming, Colorado—"

"Utah and Nevada," she finished for him. "What? They pay you mileage in addition to the bounty? Maybe you can use your spoils to buy a newer car."

"I like this one just fine."

The irritating crack about his car sent a pure dose of adrenaline straight through Micah and he cut the conversation short. Though the recharge probably wouldn't last long, he felt as if he could handle anything.

Even Angela Dragon.

FIGHTING GUILT over her last dig, Angela took refuge in Mariscano's phone directory as, finally free of rush-hour traffic, they picked up speed.

As he had on the calendar, Mariscano had identified his contacts using initials rather than full names. And the few times two people had the same initials, he'd used a first or nickname to distinguish one from the other. Encryptions had also been added to many of the entries, though it was useless to speculate on their meanings. That would take more concentration than she was capable of at the moment.

In the process of scanning the directory, Angela kept an eye out for her own initials...as well as Kaminsky's. Better to be too suspicious than gullible.

But apparently neither of them had made the little black book.

Eyes hooded, she glanced his way. Though he still appeared fatigued, his movements were injected with a newfound energy. She guessed he'd gotten his second wind. While tempted to study him for a while, she had work to do.

But a while later, halfway through the directory with nothing to show for her trouble, Angela began to lose heart. Doing little more than going through the motions, she scanned rather than fully read pages. She'd finished the last entry and was ready to close the cover on her disappointment when something hit her.

She backed up to *W*.

"W.W.," she read, then stared at the unusual entry directly below.

A single name.

"Am I supposed to understand that?" Kaminsky growled, obviously more aware of her than he'd seemed.

"Mariscano's calendar—his appointment with me was noted. And so was another later that evening. *W., Mir.* That could be the person in Las Vegas who carried out his plans."

"How do you know his other meeting was in Vegas? After leaving your office, Mariscano could have gotten on a plane for anywhere."

"True." She tapped the page. "But someone named Wily has a Las Vegas phone number. And I'd bet his last name begins with *W*, too."

Kaminsky glanced her way, his expression a combination of surprise and regard. "And I figured you took me on a wild-goose chase."

She didn't admit she'd been figuring the same.

Elated that the chance they'd taken could be duly rewarded, she said, "We have to get off this tollway so I can find a telephone. I just saw a sign that said there's an oasis two miles up the road."

"We're not getting off again."

She felt her temper stir. "Is stopping to find a telephone too much to ask?"

He reached into one of his many vest pockets. "Found." From it he pulled a cell phone and held it out to her. "No gadget cracks."

"I promise."

Never so thrilled at hearing a dial tone, she quickly punched in the number. Two rings and she had a connection.

"Desert Deals, where the savings are so hot they sizzle!" came the nasal tones of the receptionist. "How can I help you?"

"I'd like to speak to Wily."

"Who?"

"Wily...his last name escapes me," she fibbed. "But I think it starts with another *W*."

"Do you know the name of his sales associate?"

"Excuse me?"

"He's here to buy a car, right?"

"No." At least, she assumed he hadn't been a customer. "You have no employee by that name?"

"I'm sorry."

"So am I." Hanging up, she said, "Maybe I dialed wrong." She punched in the numbers more carefully the second time.

"Desert Deals—"

Angela clicked off. "Great. I dialed right. The number's wrong."

"Who did you get?"

"A car dealer. Wait a minute. Desert Deals...why does that sound familiar?"

"Some late-night television commercial with a stiff-backed owner hawking his wares and telling you to 'come on down for the best deal in town'?"

"You're right." She could visualize the owner, a short man in his mid-fifties, standing in front of a Joshua tree, an identifier of sorts for the dealership. "Ever hear of Frank Gonnella?"

"Doesn't ring a bell."

"He's quite the salesman. Expensively dressed. Moderately macho. And definitely connected."

Chapter Five

"So the owner of Desert Deals is a mobster?" Kaminsky asked.

"Retired. At least, supposedly. Gonnella used to be a small-time hood with an operation in a motel on the outskirts of the city."

Because of her father, Angela had learned far more than she'd ever wanted to about underworld figures.

"What kind of operation?"

"In addition to the legal gambling? Prostitution, which you may know is illegal in Las Vegas and Clark County, though it never has been wiped out. As far as I remember, Gonnella was never indicted, probably because he got out while the going was good." Not that she made a point of keeping track. "Now he owns one of the biggest car dealerships in Nevada. I have no clue as to what he was doing in between."

"Hmm. A lot of money goes through his business— who's to say it's all clean? And *you've* been indicted for supposed money laundering."

His sounding as though he believed in her innocence surprised Angela. "If Gonnella still works for the organization, a car dealership would be a perfect cover for a clean-up operation. And if he *was* doing what I was accused of...that *would* be quite a coincidence.''

"A coincidence...or Frank Gonnella is Joey Mariscano's Las Vegas connection. Wily could work for him personally rather than for the dealership—"

"Which would explain why the receptionist didn't recognize the name." Hope renewed, she was already thumbing through the phone directory. She stopped at *G*. "Except Frank Gonnella's not listed."

"Which doesn't automatically eliminate him. We have no way of knowing Mariscano's record-keeping system. He likes to make his notes in code. For all we know, part of that system could be to keep track of flunkies rather than bosses."

"True." Now she was scanning the black book for other Las Vegas numbers, just in case she'd missed one. "But how to find out if Gonnella's involved for certain...?"

Barely aware when they crossed the state line, Angela found herself considering the correlation between Mariscano, Wily, Gonnella and her indictment. Her mind went around and around with the possibilities, drifting further and further away from her task. Therefore, she temporarily gave up on the directory and set it down until she could be more focused. She was stewing over her helplessness in getting more information on either Frank Gonnella or this Wily character.

Reaching Nevada would probably take a few days of solid, forget-the-speed-limit driving.

And Kaminsky was barely pushing the speed limit now, Angela noticed. She glanced around. Others were driving likewise, though there wasn't enough traffic to slow anyone down. Weird. As if the state line was some kind of magical barrier after which everyone obeyed the law.

State line…law…both reminded Angela her fate lay in someone else's hands.

Once Kaminsky turned her over to the authorities, she feared that fate rested in a jail cell. And even if she was free to investigate on her own behalf, the crooks would have plenty of time to regroup and cover their tracks.

If not set another trap for her.

They'd tried to shut her up permanently once. What was to stop them from finishing the job? And what more could she do in her situation other than call out the cavalry?

Her father being the logical choice.

She'd rather go to jail, Angela thought stubbornly, wanting nothing to do with the man who'd betrayed them all. Besides, she'd taken a position, and once she made up her mind about something really important, she couldn't be budged. She no longer called Tomas Dragonetti "Father." As a matter of fact, she no longer voluntarily spoke to him at all. And if forced to by circumstances—mostly so as not to upset her mother more than she had to—she did so coolly and without any form of address.

He knew how she felt, and she wouldn't give him the satisfaction of crawling to him for help.

But she could ask someone else….

Aware they were pulling off the road, she noted the truck stop ahead. Several transport trucks were parked in front of a restaurant topped by a billboard.

"Fueling up?" she asked, the giant Cheese sign making her stomach growl.

"Us and the car. Hungry?"

"Now that you mention it…" She was so hungry she

could eat a snake. Raw. "I thought you meant to drive straight through without so much as a pit stop."

"I *am* human."

A human who was nearly running on empty, she guessed. What she said was "I hadn't noticed."

If she were smart, she would find a way to take advantage of his weakness. She'd vowed to use him and lose him, and why should she give up on that plan? Because he seemed to be on her side? She'd lost her naiveté along with her father. Being sympathetic to her plight—not that Kaminsky had even admitted that much—didn't mean he would be willing to forfeit his reward for bringing her in.

Eating would give him a temporary boost, but it wouldn't replace sleep. He'd have to get some shut-eye soon. And when he did, she needed to be ready....

Heartened by the thought, she realized her mouth was already watering as delicious odors drifted from the restaurant. Food certainly would fuel her. And truckers knew all the best places to eat.

"The car can wait," Kaminsky said, parking between two trucks, the Thunderbird a dwarf among the giants. "You look like you can't."

"Am I drooling?"

"Lusting might be a better word."

The flesh along her neck got goose bumped, but Angela refused to be baited. Getting out of the car with difficulty equal to that she'd had the last time, she noticed several pairs of curious eyes turn her way.

The wedding gown.

A wandering bride might be an odd sight in the city, but out here on the road, she had to be some kind of spectacle. That would have to change if she ever wanted to get away from Kaminsky. Unfortunately, she had neither cash nor a single credit card on her to buy new clothes. Not knowing she'd be kidnapped, she'd trusted that all her valuables would be safe in the fashion show's dressing room.

And even if she could get her hands on Kaminsky's things—assuming he'd brought a change of clothing—they certainly wouldn't fit her.

She'd have to deal with the gown. Tone it down. Make it work to her advantage. The garment was ruined, anyway. Considering how the material around her legs and feet constricted her movement, she'd start with the skirt.

Inside, they passed the counter filled with nut-covered cheese logs and a display of cakes and pies and big wedges of watermelon. Angela's stomach rumbled insistently. She hurried to catch up to Kaminsky as everyone in the room turned to gawk at her.

"Is this all right?" he asked.

The Formica-topped table and vinyl booth he indicated were identical to all the others in the room.

"It's clean." She took a seat. "I'd buy, but I don't happen to have my wallet on me."

"I can afford anything you can put away."

She considered that a challenge. "You're on."

As he slid onto the bench opposite her, he said, "One thing before we order. You'll have to promise that when we're done here, you'll leave with me of your own free will." Emphatically, he added, "No fuss."

She couldn't help herself. "Don't you know a starving woman would promise anything for food?" When he scowled at her, she rolled her eyes. "Oh, lighten up, Kaminsky. You think I want to be stuck in Nowhere, Wisconsin, without a plugged nickel to my name? Besides, we have a deal. I already promised that if you took me to Mariscano's, I'd go with you voluntarily.''

Only, she hadn't said how far.

The lack of money was a kink in any plan she might make, however, even if she intended to hitch a ride to civilization. And knowing what she'd have to do to get her hands on some cash didn't sit well. Ethics was one of her strong suits. She respected the law.

She wondered how many more laws she would have to break before she got herself out of this mess.

Two glasses slid onto the table, water sloshing over their rims. A gum-chewing, bleached-blond waitress of indeterminate age arched her penciled-in eyebrows as she thoroughly inspected the wedding gown.

''What can I get ya, honey?''

''Four eggs, basted,'' Angela began. ''Hash browns and a pecan roll. Make that two. Orange juice. A piece of watermelon.'' Aware that the man footing the bill was pulling a face, she added, ''And a side order of pancakes.''

''Breakfast meat?'' the waitress asked. ''Bacon, sausage, ham?''

She met Kaminsky's piercing gaze with one of her own. ''Yes.''

''Which?''

''All. I'll decide on dessert later.''

''You got it, honey.'' The other woman's tone was more than a tad disbelieving. She snapped her gum as she turned the page on her order pad. ''The two of you sharing everything?''

Angela wasn't thinking of food when she said, ''A whole lot more than I'd like.''

Micah added, ''Double the order—only scramble my

eggs. And don't forget the coffee. Bring the whole pot and leave it.''

"All rightie.''

Snapping her gum several times in succession, the waitress left to place their order.

Angela rose. "I need to use the facilities.''

She covertly picked up a knife, but Kaminsky's hand quickly covered hers. Jolted by the unexpected contact, she plopped back down.

"What's that for?'' he demanded. "Plan to skewer me when I turn my back?''

"Don't tempt me.'' For some reason, she suddenly had trouble breathing. "The knife is to minimize my eye-catching ensemble and therefore *our* visibility...unless you expect me to rip this dress apart with my teeth.''

Reluctantly he let go of her hand; she was able to breathe normally again.

"Don't try anything,'' he warned her. "I'll be watching the door. And if you're not back in five minutes, I'll come in after you.''

Seriously thinking about staying inside for six minutes just to see what he would do, she asked, "Did you forget about the window?''

"I checked it on the way in. Glass block.''

He had the audacity to smirk at her.

Head high, Angela rose and made her way across the room, the knife concealed in the folds of her skirt so she wouldn't draw even more attention to herself. For once she wished she could blend into the wallpaper. Or in this case the landlord-green paint. Curious stares followed her every step of the way. She'd never been so glad to get inside a ladies' room, even though this one probably hadn't seen a renovation since the war. World War I, she decided.

At least the facilities were clean, in addition to functional.

Once refreshed, Angela faced herself in the mirror, saluted the dress and began the desecration. Shucking the full underslip was the easy part—rolled tight, it even fit in the recently emptied garbage can. Using a butter knife to rip through the outer layers of the skirt was another proposition, especially since she was still wearing the gown. Getting out of it herself would be too much trouble under these conditions—particularly since. her lifelong dream of becoming a contortionist had never panned out.

In the middle of her struggle with the back of the skirt, the door opened. Thinking the bounty hunter really *had* followed her, she started. When she saw the teenager dragging a toddler by the hand, she relaxed.

"Hey, congrats on the big day." Then the girl's gaze settled on the dull knife hacking through the delicate material. "Uh...I think."

"Thanks." Fighting with a stubborn lace frill, Angela nearly growled her response.

Wide-eyed, the teen lifted the toddler and scurried away. A moment later the stillness was punctured by short bursts of smothered giggles emanating from the middle stall.

Angela ignored the irritating sound and worked as quickly as she could. The raggedy hem of the skirt dipped and rose in choppy waves a few inches below her knees. Not pretty, but she certainly felt better, as if she'd been freed from quicksand.

She considered tearing out the sleeves, as well, but she probably wouldn't be able to make a run for it until later that evening when the air would be cool. She settled for ridding herself of the drippy lace at her elbows, then the stuff around the bodice. She checked the mirror and saw that she'd managed to lower the neckline enough to reveal the swell of her breasts. Now she merely looked like a debutante at a garden party instead of a bride, Angela thought wryly.

A debutante with a hole in her head. She quickly adjusted her hair, covering the bald spot that seemed to grow larger each time she saw it.

The dress still drew a reaction from both customers and staff as she made her way back to the table now mounded with food. All the customers continued to be mesmerized by the sight of her. Kaminsky's eyes were especially appreciative, the blue deepening to the glow of the night sky following sunset. He seemed to be looking at her not as a fugitive but as a woman.

And the primal woman inside her responded, making her a little slow on the uptake when he asked, "For me? You shouldn't have."

She blinked, noting that a tiny dimple creased his right cheek when he smiled. "Don't worry—I didn't."

Slowly she sat and chastised herself. She had to keep sharp. On top of things. She needed to regroup, to regain control of her life. Always a winner, she planned to stay that way...no matter what she had to do.

The last thought stuck in her craw. What *would* she have to do?

"I thought you were hungry."

She snapped out of her thoughts and inhaled the mouthwatering aromas. "Starving."

What followed was nothing short of a competition. Bite for bite. Sip for sip. Swallow for swallow. Forget conversation, polite or otherwise. Her mother had always called her a healthy eater—a lumberjack was more like it. Luckily, she had a cooperative metabolism. She'd never eaten *this* much at a single sitting, though. And from the size of him, she guessed Kaminsky could go her one better.

Halfway through the meal, when he showed signs of slowing down, she was mightily relieved and allowed herself to do the same.

He leaned against his booth back and washed down half a cup of coffee in one gulp. "So...you never did say why Mariscano set you up. How did you get yourself into this fix in the first place?"

She didn't miss the intimation that he figured it was her fault. "Probably by not being cooperative."

"Big surprise."

"Mariscano wanted to buy into our business and I said 'No, thanks.'"

"What would a big-time entrepreneur want with a company that specializes in weddings?"

"You mean a crook," she said flatly. "And that was the same question I asked myself."

"So what was your conclusion?"

"That he thought I had hidden interests—"

"Because of your father," he interjected.

"—which I don't. And my father has absolutely no hand in the business."

"Okay, what about this—how about giving Mariscano the benefit of the doubt as far as your troubles with the law are concerned—"

"Why should I?" It was her turn to interrupt.

"And see if you can't come up with someone else who has reason to want you out of the way."

Out of the way...

He made it sound as though she were an inconvenience. Or a stumbling block.

Frowning at the last, she said, "Fingering Mariscano wasn't a snap judgment on my part."

But he continued to play devil's advocate. "Maybe Mariscano only wanted to make sure his daughter had the wedding of the century and thought he could do that better if he owned a piece of the action."

"That must be why he threatened me when I turned him down," Angela said, yet remembering the way he'd looked at DeeDee. "No doubt he assumes his daughter will always love him, no matter what he does."

Face wreathed in the strangest expression, Kaminsky said, "It's hard to stop loving someone, even when you know the things they do are wrong."

If he meant she must still love *her* father, he was way off base. About to slap him with a tart response, Angela bit her tongue before she could make a fool of herself. Of course he'd meant DeeDee and *her* father.

Instead, she merely said, "Don't generalize. What's true for little DeeDee isn't necessarily true for everyone." Especially not for her.

"All right. So we'll make it a given that Mariscano's motives weren't pure," he went on. "He assumes your father is part of your operation because he knows you're a family person. He can see that from the way you all worked together to build Here Comes the Bride."

Angela wondered if everyone in the country knew every detail of her life. "Right. Me, my mother and my siblings."

"Your father *couldn't* be around."

He *was* talking about her. Any appetite she might have left vanished.

"We wouldn't have had to build a new business if he

had been! And, please, don't make it sound nice, like he was on a vacation or something. He was incarcerated. In prison, *where he belonged!*'' she added vehemently.

''You're bitter.''

''Realistic.''

''And still trying to make up for it.''

His conclusion stunned her. ''You mean make up for *him?* Not hardly. He's not worth it. I'm not one to let *myself* down. Or those I love.'' She spelled it out for him. ''My mother, Benedict and Petra.''

''I'm sure your father never meant to hurt you. What he did for a living didn't affect his feelings for his family.''

''What he did was illegal!''

Expression odd, he said, ''No one's born a crook, but anyone can be influenced by circumstances. Your father made a big mistake—''

''A *mistake?*'' she echoed in disbelief.

''In judgment,'' Kaminsky clarified, ''when he chose to hook up with the wrong people. Unless you believe he's evil.''

''I never said that.'' Angela had thought she was immune to the confused feelings the bounty hunter was stirring up inside. She spoke over the lump in her throat. ''Besides, mistakes can be corrected.''

''Sometimes. If one wrong move doesn't lead to another and another and another until they trap a person. Whatever your father's situation, his wrong choices had nothing to do with how much he cared for his family.''

''His choices *ruined* his family.''

''Did they? Or did they make you stronger?''

What business did Kaminsky have dredging up her past? And why did he seem to be on her father's side?

Unable to tolerate more, Angela donned the poker

face she used when dealing with unpleasant business is-
sues. "Time's flying. I'm ready to leave."

He stared at her as if trying to figure out whether or
not he should press the issue. Then he recouped. "Your
food—"

"Is cold. Can we go now?"

Thankfully, he didn't argue, merely picked up the
check and retrieved his wallet. Angela stared at the worn
leather. When he opened it, she got a glimpse of a couple
of fifties nestled behind the smaller bills. He had to be
carrying nearly two hundred dollars in cash.

She was considering ways to get her hands on that
money when her pulse suddenly surged.

Stealing—no matter how insignificant an amount—
was against everything she believed in. And yet she
wouldn't get far without funds, and the need to put distance between them as soon as possible plagued her.

Food had charged the man's batteries. He appeared
vital. Intense. But the truth lay in his eyes. The weariness
lurking within. The dark hollows below. As desperately
as he needed sleep, his newfound energy wouldn't last
long. His blood sugar was just waiting to nose-dive.

And when he finally crashed, she'd be waiting to take
advantage.

As for the money…

Angela would find a way to *borrow* some. She chose
to consider the money a loan, whether or not she had
Micah Kaminsky's consent. Vowing to repay every single penny, even the breakfast check, relaxed her scruples
a tad.

"Maybe you'd better use the facilities before we get
back on the road," he suggested. "It may be some time
before we stop again."

"Not necessary," she returned stiffly.

"You're sure?"

He leaned across the table and cupped her chin with firm fingers, then rubbed the corner of her mouth with his thumb. Surprised, she couldn't move for a moment as the rough pad stroked the soft flesh of her lower lip....

Realizing she was letting him get to her on a physical as well as an emotional level, Angela jerked her head back. "What do you think you're doing?"

"Egg yolk. Though I do enjoy an enthusiastic eater, I don't need to be reminded of the menu."

He held out his thumb so she could see the bit of crusted yellow he'd removed.

Heat warming her neck, she flew to her feet. "Fine. I'll be right back."

"You won't find me here. The car needs gas, remember."

"Outside, then."

"Don't—"

"Try anything," she finished for him. "I know. I know."

She couldn't wait to get out of his company.

For good.

MICAH SAVORED watching Angela flounce across the room, the heat of anger and embarrassment adding a provocative cadence to her movements.

Also glad that he'd be rid of her for a few minutes, he rose and approached the cash register. Now he could try making the call again. He'd had the perfect opportunity while she'd been butchering that dress. Too bad he hadn't been able to get through.

Handing the check to the waitress with enough money to include a generous tip, he whipped out of the restaurant. The place was jumping with vehicles—a variety of cars and four-by-fours, as well as the eighteen-wheelers. He took a good look around. It wouldn't do to let down his guard. But all he saw were truckers and ordinary people. Several families on summer vacations.

The cell phone was in his hand even as he started the car. He punched the number by memory as he pulled over to a recently vacated gas pump.

One ring...two...

"Yeah" came the familiar voice on the other end. "Talk to me."

"I have her." He left the car and removed the cap to the gas tank, his gaze constantly on the move, addressing the people around him. "We're on the way."

"About time. I expected to hear from you before this."

"We ran into a hitch," Micah informed him. "Unforeseen trouble."

"What did she do?"

Despite the seriousness of the situation, he had to grin. Angela Dragon was predictable in her unpredictability. "Not *her*...though you were right. She isn't easy to handle."

"But you'll manage."

"As agreed."

"Good. How soon can I expect delivery?"

"I'm not sure. A couple of days." He started the gas pump. "We'd be on the westbound train if we hadn't run into that hitch at Union Station." Micah tried not to sound ticked when he added, "You didn't say anything about danger."

"I didn't think I had to spell it out for you!" the other man growled. "Hey, you ever heard of flying?"

"On one of those things with wings?" Micah laced his tone with sarcasm to cover his true reaction. "Too obvious. I said I'd do it, but I do it my way or not at all.''

The long pause made him wonder if he'd gone too far until the other man said, "However you can make it work."

That settled, Micah quickly went over the itinerary he had in mind…assuming everything went like clockwork.

"You're taking the scenic route?"

"Any objections?"

"Yeah, I got objections…but I trust your judgment. Just get her back."

From the corner of his eye Micah spotted movement at the restaurant door, which swung open, raggedy white skirts preceding the wearer.

"She's coming. I have to go."

"Keep in touch."

Having thrown his vest over the bucket seat, Micah slipped the phone into one of the pockets. Then he returned to nurse the gas nozzle and watched Angela stalk over to him. He noticed she'd unpinned her remaining curls. The breeze whipped the hair around her face and played havoc with his imagination.

He could picture the sea of dark waves splayed across a pillow next to him.…

Though he could tell she was still angry, she was doing her best not to show it. But the pleasant smile she pasted on her lips served to warn him she was up to something. He narrowed his gaze and stared at her suspiciously. She smiled harder and slid into the passenger seat.

The pump clicked. The rush of gas stopped.

"Tank's full," he announced. "We're off as soon as I pay."

"I'll be here."

Would she?

Micah's well-honed instincts told him Angela was getting ready to jump again. Something about that smile...the shuttered eyes...the way she held her body.

Where in the world did she think she was going to hide from him dressed so conspicuously?

Not to mention that she had no identification and no money.

Sauntering to the cashier's window where a line had already formed ahead of him, he kept one eye on the Thunderbird. Angela sat still as a statue. For now. But what if she figured out some way to unlock the door....

All she had to do was stick one toe out onto the pavement and he'd be all over her.

And then she'd pay the consequences.

ANGELA BARELY WAITED until the bounty hunter's back was to her before acting. Keeping an eye on him, she sneaked a hand over to his discarded vest and the pocket where he stashed the cell phone.

A little time out of his company had given her the opportunity to think things through. To decide she needed to call in the cavalry despite wanting to do things herself. Micah Kaminsky had put a kink in her plans, and now the odds were against her succeeding alone.

Besides, she was only going to ask Douglas to get her some information. It wasn't as if she was involving him physically or putting him at risk, she thought, guilt niggling at her. She wouldn't do that to the man she...was dating. Honest with herself, she knew that while she'd had some reflective thoughts about their future together, Douglas was far more serious about their relationship than she was.

Angela figured this to be another consequence of her

father's mistaken choices. She'd never been able to trust a man enough to open her heart.

Leaving her hand lower than the dash, she watched Kaminsky while her fingers flew over the key pad. Only three people ahead of him. She would have to make this quick. She shifted to her side and lowered her cheek to the seat back, slipping the receiver between her ear and the cushion. She hoped the bounty hunter would assume she was merely trying to get comfortable...and that the fall of her hair camouflaged the phone as she'd planned when she'd freed it.

The phone rang several times. Disappointment at not finding Douglas at home edged through her. She tried his cellular phone number. Two rings and he answered.

"Yes?"

Relief swept through her. "It's Angela."

"Sweetheart, where are you?" His voice was intense with worry. "Marcie said you hadn't been at work all day, and I've left several messages on your machine."

Checking on the bounty hunter, she said, "I'm on my way back from Chicago."

Only two people left ahead of him.

"Dear Lord, you went after Mariscano yourself! I was afraid of this. I would have gone with you. You're all right, aren't you?"

"I'm fine and I didn't tell you because I didn't want to involve you. Only now I need to."

"What time is your flight? I'll meet you, of course."

"No flight...for the moment. A bounty hunter named Micah Kaminsky is escorting me the long way home."

Her mouth went dry when he glanced her way, but apparently her plan was working, for he turned back as the next customer stepped up to the window.

"Where are you now?"

"Some truck stop in Wisconsin. Kaminsky plans to take U.S. 90 across Minnesota and South Dakota, but I hope to be long gone before we cross the state line."

"Darling, don't do anything foolish," Douglas begged. "A recovery agent will expect his reward. He may shoot you rather than let you escape. Say, have you offered him money to let you go?"

"Among other things," she muttered. That he was so worried about her made her uncomfortable. "Unfortunately, he seems to be incorruptible."

"That is too bad. What is it you want me to do?"

"Contact the private investigator Jenkins hired. Have him find out what he can about Frank Gonnella and a wild card—Wily something."

"Who are these people?"

She was so involved in giving him a quick recap that she didn't realize anything was wrong until a *beep* alerted her. The next thing she knew, the door flew open, a hand gripped her upper arm and she was hauled out of the vehicle to face one furious bounty hunter.

Chapter Six

"I knew you were up to something!" Feeling as if he were hanging on to a writhing pit viper, Micah grabbed the cell phone and brought it to his ear. "Hello? Who is this?"

He listened to silence followed by a dial tone.

Angela continued to fight him. Futilely. Though he wasn't hurting her, he had an ungiving grip on her arm directly above the elbow. And he wasn't ready to release her yet.

"Let go of me!" she demanded, threatening him with a balled fist.

"I wouldn't do that, if I were you," he warned her, aware that the woman filling her gas tank next to them was staring. "Remember the last time."

"You mean when you *hit* me?"

Her eyes shifted to a muscle-bound teenage boy who was cleaning his windshield, as if she wanted to make certain he'd heard. An effective strategy. The kid's jaw dropped and he stopped what he was doing.

Micah asked, "Who did you call?" more reasonably than he was feeling.

Through gritted teeth she insisted, "It's none of your business."

"Everything you do is my business until I get you back to Nevada."

"Let me go! *Now!*"

At the shouted demand, several more heads turned their way. Great. Exactly what they needed—witnesses who could identify them.

Certain Angela couldn't keep a low profile if one was handed to her on a silver platter, Micah insisted, "I'll let you go...as soon as you tell me who you called and why." In reality he was beginning to feel pressured to give in before some interfering idiot summoned the cops.

Suddenly stopping her struggle, Angela caved in. "Oh, all right. I wanted someone to know I was *still alive.*"

Her implication that *he* might have tried to kill her didn't get by him. He clenched his jaw. "Who?"

"If you must know..." In a much lower tone she said, "My fiancé, Douglas Neff. Call him back if you don't believe me." She raised her voice once more. "Now that I've made the big confession, you can release my arm."

Thankful they'd be rid of the unwanted attention, Micah finally let go.

Fiancé?

Some poor fool actually wanted to spend the rest of his life with this harridan?

Wondering exactly how much she'd told the man, Micah figured he could wait until they were on the road to find out. "Okay, get back in the car."

"Not until you apologize."

"For what?"

Rubbing her arm where he'd been holding it—as if he'd hurt her!—she said, "For being a boor."

"You mean for not letting you get away with anything."

The woman who'd been pumping gas next to them replaced the nozzle in its holder and remained next to the pump, obviously in no hurry to leave. She frowned at him over the glasses perched at the tip of her nose.

"Is that any way to talk to your new bride?"

Bride?

Then it hit him. The wedding gown...what was left of it. The stranger thought they'd just gotten married. He decided to play along.

"We had a little misunderstanding, ma'am, that's all. And I never really hit her," he said earnestly. "She's into kinky stuff. Spanking." He turned to Angela, figuring those were poisonous darts she glared at him. "Isn't that right, darling? Now, would you *please* get in the car?"

Arms crossed over her chest, she sweetly demanded, "Apology first."

"But we have to get on the road...*Angel.*" He didn't miss the scowl she aimed at him because of the nickname. "I insist."

"Hold on, sonny." An elderly woman waving a wicked-looking cane joined the protester at the pump. "You can't treat your new wife like she's your chattel. And on your wedding day, for heaven's sake. Shame on you!"

"Honey, you made a big mistake marrying this bozo, but it's not too late." A tough-looking woman trucker stopped barely a yard away. "If you don't want to go with the brute, say the word." She wiped her greasy hands on her overalls and glared at him. "You can hitch a ride back to civilization with me."

"Thanks for the offer. Maybe I'll take you up on it if he continues to behave so badly." Angela stared at him expectantly. "Well?"

Micah knew when he was licked. All he wanted was to get away from the place and fast, so he said, "You're right. I apologize."

"That's it?" the teenage boy asked. "Heck, if I didn't do better than that, my girlfriend wouldn't even speak to me for days."

Thinking he wouldn't mind if Angela didn't speak to him all the way back to Nevada—he was tempted to gag her himself—Micah kept up the just-married charade.

"I was wrong, *Angel.* I won't jump to conclusions again." He gave the small crowd a shamefaced look. "I really thought she was calling her old boyfriend to make him feel better. He tried to break us up...and right before the wedding, too." Then back to Angela. "All right?"

"Better."

Still, she didn't budge. Obviously she didn't appreciate his creativity.

And Micah didn't appreciate her stubbornness. What was the point? Did she need the attention of everyone in the county? His aggravation quotient soaring right off the Richter scale, he finally lost it.

"I don't know how else to say it with words."

Snaking an arm around her waist, Micah pulled Angela to him, intent on ending the confrontation the only way she'd left him. The curves of her body pressed up against his gave him quite a jolt. She appeared equally affected. Her almond eyes widened and her mouth opened.

Before she could utter a single word of protest, he locked his lips to hers.

Angela was so taken aback at the unexpected assault that any protest—physical or otherwise—was impossible. She froze while Kaminsky's lips worked magic on hers. Before she knew what was happening, he was exploring her mouth thoroughly, and she wasn't doing a thing to stop him.

Stop him.

Right. That's what she should be doing.

Pulse threading unevenly, she put out her hands to shove him away. Contact. But rather than pushing, she grabbed his arms and pressed her nails into them. His bare flesh pulsed and his skin was warm beneath her fingertips. Sensation shot along her nerves, all the way up to her head.

A lovely floaty feeling filled her and Angela closed her eyes.

For a moment all the fear and uncertainty of the past months receded. For a moment she felt protected and safe. For a moment she was fully alive, a whole woman again.

Or perhaps for the first time in her life.

She responded with wonder and enthusiasm...returning his kiss...clinging to his muscular upper arms...pressing closer until an urgency uncoiled deep in her belly.

Her pulse raced and her heated blood rushed through her head, making her ears ring. The longer she kissed him, the louder the sound grew. Louder and clearer. Finally she realized her mistake: rather than the rush of her pulse, she was listening to clapping.

Applause!

What in the world was she doing?

Appalled at her own behavior, she freed her mouth and shoved at the bounty hunter. He stepped back, locking gazes with her, seemingly as surprised as she.

Unnerved, too, if she was any judge.

"We should go now," Angela muttered.

Sliding back into the passenger seat, she tried to avoid

meeting the eyes of anyone in the crowd gathered around them. An impossible feat. She was trapped, like a deer by headlights. And nearly every person was smiling. Even the woman trucker who'd offered her the ride to civilization wore a resigned expression.

What was wrong with them? Could anyone be fooled if they thought romance was somehow involved?

Anyone but her.

There was nothing romantic about that kiss—Kaminsky's ploy to smooth things over.

And she'd been a sap to go along with it.

Unwilling to give him the satisfaction of thinking her response had been anything but an act, she adopted a smug smile as he got into the car. Unable to miss it, he scowled in return, started the engine and shot off.

She expected him to say something about the kiss as soon as they pulled away from the truck stop. He didn't. She waited, tense and wary. Miles rolled by, seemingly at a crawl since—like every other driver on the Wisconsin road—he refused to challenge the speed limit.

The silence between them grew heavy.

What was his game?

Did he think he had her number? That he had her under control because she was attracted to him? He wasn't even giving her the opportunity to go a couple of rounds over what had happened between them.

Perhaps nothing had happened for him.

Honest with herself, Angela admitted *she* had felt something. Rational now, she put her response to the heat of the moment, initially sparked by her temper. Not to mention the danger lurking in the background. She could never be interested seriously in a man who made his living off other people's misfortune.

Prickly, she couldn't leave it alone and pretend it

never happened. She longed to make him wish he'd never so much as thought of touching her.

"I didn't know you had it in you, Kaminsky," she began in a conversational tone. "That was some act you put on for the folks back there."

"Call me a quick thinker."

There were a lot of things she'd like to call him— *quick thinker* not being among them.

"Better yet," he added, "call me Micah. Kaminsky's a little formal now that we've gotten so close."

He did think he had her! And listen to his tone...how normal...how unaffected. The exact opposite of the way she was feeling. Her emotions were roller-coasting between wanting him to kiss her again...and wanting to punch him in the kisser.

Pride stinging, Angela said, "If you insist. Good show, *Micah.*"

Having thought of him as Kaminsky for so long, she felt that switching to Micah made him seem like a different man altogether. But of course he was the same unscrupulous bounty hunter who'd thrown her over his shoulder and spoiled her plans.

She kept her voice neutral. "Luckily we didn't have too sophisticated an audience."

He glanced at her. "How so?"

"Why, anyone with a critical eye would have seen through what you let pass for a hot kiss. That's why I gave it my best shot—so that it'd look real anyway."

Though he was staring straight forward, she could see him narrow his gaze.

"And here I would have sworn you couldn't help yourself," he countered.

She laughed softly, convincingly, and glanced out at

the gently rolling landscape beyond the passenger window. Lots of places to run to; no place to hide.

"Men do tend to fool themselves when it comes to their sexual prowess."

Tension, thick and heavy, suddenly charged the atmosphere around her. Angela smiled to herself, able to tell that he wasn't quite sure...

Good.

"Besides," she murmured, giving him a direct look, "if they hadn't been fooled by the gown, they would have realized that a real lady...while intrigued...would never get serious with your type of man."

His fingers wound so tightly around the steering wheel that his knuckles turned white. "What's that supposed to mean? That you're better than me?"

"Well...I don't like measuring people's worth...but since you asked...you are a little...*crude* around the edges."

He chewed on that for a moment before launching a counterattack. "At least I'm not half-witted. I hope you're happy with your big play for attention from the locals, Dragonlady. If someone comes after us in this direction, dozens of people can recognize our photos or description."

The second time he'd called her by the unflattering nickname. Dragonlady or Angel—she wasn't certain which rankled more.

"Not quite that many," she argued. "And it certainly was not my fault."

"I would have sworn you were the one who said I hit you—"

"The truth, as I remember."

"And intimated that I was a killer."

"I half thought so before you identified yourself as a

bounty hunter. And how do I know you're not?'' She gave him a superior smile. ''Would you rather I'd suggested you were a *lady*killer?''

Obviously not wanting to go there, he didn't answer.

And Angela gained only temporary pleasure from having one-upped him.

That was the trouble with going after someone with talons out, no matter how much the other person deserved it. Once the satisfaction wore off, it left her feeling empty and mean-spirited. Not that she made a practice of going for the jugular. But when someone cornered her, made her feel like less of a person, she couldn't help herself.

Dragonlady...

Is that what she'd become?

Angela disliked the implication. Something else to discuss with her therapist, assuming she ever had the chance to reclaim her real life.

The sun hung low in the western sky, and she'd been up since before dawn. Dawn two time zones away. She'd had only a few hours of sleep before rising to catch her plane to Chicago. All day she'd been running on adrenaline pumped by belief in her ability to accomplish anything she set her mind to.

Now doubt assailed her and she felt as tired as her captor looked. Dealing with Mariscano was one thing. But what chance did she have of clearing her name if the organization was really backing him?

How could she have been foolish enough not to consider that very likely scenario?

Alone in a world filled with people she couldn't trust—being held against her will by a man who was ready and willing to turn her over to the authorities in exchange for a bankroll—Angela was finding it difficult to believe that, this time, she had any chance to come out on top.

LONG SHADOWS FINGERED the corners of his office as he ruminated on the unexpected turn his plan had taken.

"She's proving even more difficult than expected. She's not an easy scapegoat."

He noted his associate's quick change of expression—a moment's panic quickly disguised, perhaps? Or could that have been pity?

"How much longer is she going to be on the loose?"

"She should never have been allowed to cross the state line in the first place!" He continued watching for any sign of weakness, but the other man covered well. "At least we know they're on the road in Wisconsin—"

"What the hell are they doing wandering around Cheddarland, anyway?" the other man muttered, then popped out of his chair and began pacing. "Taking in the damn sights?"

"Not for long," he said calmly, though in a perverse way the challenge stimulated him. Things that came too easily never seemed truly worthwhile. "And we know they'll head across country on U.S. 90—"

"Which really narrows it down."

He ignored the sarcasm. "I'll dispatch a couple of men into Minneapolis on the next flight. Don't worry. They'll pick up the trail somewhere in Minnesota."

"They'd better...but if they fail?"

Staring, he calmly said, "Wily never fails. Not in the end. He's as clever as his name implies."

"Too bad you can't control him." A tense pause was followed by a stiff "Are your instructions to hold her...or to finish her off?"

"Bloodthirsty, are you?"

"You know I hate this! No one was supposed to get killed. I didn't sign up for murder!"

"Damage control can be unpleasant," he agreed. "Even if it is necessary."

In the old days, damage control had been a fact of life...not that murder had been a solution if some other means could be equally effective. This was a different world—fast paced, run by punks who had no respect, who killed because they were bored or high on drugs.

But *he* remembered how business should be conducted.

He remembered other things, too. Things that were done *for* him. *To* him. *Despite* him.

A long memory ticked like a time bomb.

One way or another, he'd finally get the satisfaction owed him.

"WHY WOULD JOEY MARISCANO want to buy into a wedding business?"

Stirring at the intrusive voice, Angela opened her eyes and stretched her spine. "We've been through all that."

For a while she'd managed to distance her mind from her situation and Micah Kaminsky. Now both problems pressed in on her in crashing clarity. Yawning, she sat up straight, amazed at the lateness of the hour. While she'd been dozing off and on, the sun had set.

"So let's do it again," Micah said.

His words instigated a fleeting memory of the kiss, but she was certain that's not what he meant. And she'd made far too big a deal of the incident.

"Like I told you, he probably assumed my father—"

"Did they have a long-distance relationship?" he interrupted impatiently. "Business?"

Rubbing at her eyes, she yawned again and wondered

how Micah had managed to stay awake without her to needle him. "Not that I'm aware of."

"Did they even know each other?"

"You'd have to ask one of them. If either would tell the truth." She sat up straighter and stared out into the glowing dusk where innumerable stars crowned a nearly full moon. A romantic night for a romantic adventure. Too bad she wasn't having one. "What difference does it make?"

"I'm trying to make sense of things. Like why Mariscano had reason to believe your father had hidden interests in Here Comes the Bride with him straight out of the joint. Or why he would even have reason to consider your father at all."

Neither had occurred to her. "I guess I don't think like a criminal."

"That's the problem," Micah said. "You need to."

Did that mean *he* thought like one?

Angela wondered how one developed that particular skill without being a criminal oneself.

"Let's forget Joey Mariscano for the moment," Micah continued, "and concentrate on what you know of Tomas Dragonetti's enemies."

Back to her father. "I was hardly more than a kid when he was locked away. How much do you expect me to remember?" Though she had to admit narrowing the field would be helpful. Surely one of his old allies wouldn't act against her.

"I don't believe you've forgotten a thing," Micah insisted. "You haven't allowed yourself to."

What he said was true.

"But I never knew the details of his business interests in the first place," she protested. "None of us did. He made sure of that."

"You never picked up on names?"

"Of course I know names." She'd made it a point to learn the various players, if after the fact. "I gave you one—Frank Gonnella. But who was friend and who was foe?" She shook her head. "It's more complicated than that. Sally Donatelli, Otto Usher, Harold Lipinski, Carmine Scudella—all serious business rivals of my father's. But enemies?" She shrugged. "I don't have a clue."

"Otto Usher?" he echoed.

Angela wondered at his odd tone. "I take it you've heard of him." When he didn't respond, she said, "He's an old man, and rumor is he's been seriously ill, so he keeps to himself. Under the circumstances—"

"What about his family?"

"His son, Norman, is a long-term guest of the governor. The daughter doesn't live in Nevada anymore." Maybe she'd fled the infamy of her family, something Angela had been tempted to do. "So what's the interest in Usher?"

"Call it instinct."

Instinct? Or something more concrete? Was Micah holding out on her? She gazed through the dark, studied his profile in silhouette, but could read nothing.

"Are you sure you don't remember anything specific about your father's connections?"

Angela hated thinking about the past, but she forced herself back in time where a vague memory stirred.

"The trial...near the end. One day Mama came home really upset about someone being in the courtroom. She said he had a lot of nerve showing his face. That he sat in the back the whole day and gloated."

"Who?"

But the rest was elusive. What she'd focused on was her mother's pain rather than the details.

"If she ever mentioned his name, I don't remember."

"Try."

Her stomach was already knotted. "I hate remembering! I hate everything about that time of my life."

"You hate your father?"

Did she?

"Shouldn't I?"

"You can hate what he did. That doesn't mean you have to hate *him.*"

"The great philosopher." Bitterness surfaced. "What do you know about it? You're not the one whose father was incarcerated, leaving his family impoverished. Your classmates didn't ridicule you and exclude you."

"That was nearly twenty years ago. Get over it."

Micah spoke so dispassionately, they might have been discussing a bad prom date. He didn't understand. He never would. And Angela didn't understand why she was wasting her time arguing about it.

"*Those* are the kind of memories you never forget," she said. "And I'm as over it as I'll ever be."

"Then I feel sorry for you."

"I don't need your pity."

"You don't have my pity, though you do have my sympathy, even if you weren't the only kid in the world who got a raw deal. But some of us learn to shelve the past and get on with our lives."

Some of us? Him, specifically?

What did he have to complain about? Wearing hand-me-down clothes or adjusting to divorce? Normal kid worries, as far as she was concerned.

Angela might have asked what he'd meant anyway, if he hadn't been beginning to sound like her therapist.

How many times had Judith suggested she needed to resolve her anger with her father before she could be truly happy? But despite all the recommendations, she'd never been able to force herself to do so.

Heading off the highway, Micah broke in to her thoughts. "Since you don't know the dynamics of the past, you'll have to ask someone who does."

"I won't involve my mother."

"I was thinking of a more direct line."

Her father, of course. "I don't want his help."

"You need it."

"I'll go to jail before I ask him for anything! He never even said he was sorry for what he did to us." She somehow got past the lump in her throat. "At least, not to me."

"Did you ever give him the chance?"

Angela clenched her jaw. Why did it sound as if he was taking her father's side again? Not wanting to continue this conversation, she was relieved when he pulled the car up in front of a motel.

Until she got a good look at the place.

The paint was peeling. A window was boarded. And the *E* in MOTEL was out.

"Choice," she murmured, assuming the bedding had to be as decrepit as the rest of the place. "Is this the best you can do?"

"No one would think of looking for 'a lady' in a place like this, now, would they?" He left the car without waiting for her comeback.

Figuring she deserved a good shot after the things she'd said to him earlier, Angela took it philosophically and waited for Micah's return.

Why did she let him get to her? He was a temporary

situation. An inconvenience. Nothing more. So what if she'd responded to his kiss? Big deal.

Her juices had been flowing from the little act she'd put on for the bystanders.

The fact that she'd done something so uncharacteristic bothered her. Why hadn't she demanded help? Or she could have left with the trucker—Micah couldn't have stopped her with all those people around.

Furthermore, she'd allowed him to draw her into painful discussions about her father that roused her anger. She'd barely expressed her feelings to Douglas, and she'd been dating *him* for several months. He respected her wishes and kept his nose out of her past.

Micah Kaminsky was a total stranger—she really didn't know a thing about him—and that's the way she wanted it, Angela told herself. What prompted him to keep at her? Thankfully, she wouldn't have to put up with his know-it-all attitude much longer.

Concentrating on being a free agent again nearly put her in a good mood. When Micah opened the passenger door a few minutes later, he was twirling a motel key around his forefinger. *A* key, as in *one*.

"Too much to think I'd get my own space."

"Too much," he agreed.

She exited the car and waited while he locked up without taking anything. Wistfully, she glanced at the vest still hanging over the back of his seat. What she wouldn't give to get her hands on that cell phone. She'd feel much more secure escaping into the night with a way to call for help if she got into real trouble.

Not that she really knew where she was.

When they entered the musty-smelling room with only one saggy double bed, and the intimacy of the accommodations struck her, she had to remind herself that she'd never sleep there, anyway.

She wrinkled her nose. "Smells awful."

Micah crossed to the air conditioner stationed below the window and flipped the switch. The appliance groaned, screeched and rattled, but finally kicked in.

The bathroom fixtures were equally well-worn. And only someone wearing hip boots would want to venture into the moldy shower. Wondering how the place was able to stay in business, she vacated the bathroom as quickly as possible.

Drawing curtains over the window, Micah said, "It'll probably take a while to cool down in here. I have some extra T-shirts in the trunk."

Imagining herself lying next to him wearing nothing but a layer of thin cotton, Angela quickly said, "I prefer the gown."

He shrugged. "It's your problem."

"It's not a problem at all," she fibbed.

The dress wasn't bad, but the corset beneath made her feel as if she were encased in a body cuff. She wondered if she'd taken a truly normal breath since donning it. Kicking off her shoes, she flopped onto the bed, which responded with a series of metallic protests.

"Great. The springs squeak," she muttered, realizing this was not a plus for her getaway plans.

"It won't keep me awake."

"I hope not...that it won't keep me awake, either," she quickly finished.

Micah flipped the wall switch so the overhead light went off. "There is a plus side to your not changing out of that thing," he said, his voice holding a hint of amusement. "We might have some trouble getting you back into it if we have to ditch the place fast."

We?

Thinking about his hands on her bare skin sent an involuntary shudder coursing through her.

And when, silhouetted by the bathroom light, he stripped off his T-shirt, Angela closed her eyes...but not before she got a breathtaking view of his naked chest. The sound of a zipper gave her a start. Unable to help herself, she peeked out through lowered lashes.

Her rationale: she needed to know where he put his jeans so she wouldn't be fumbling in the dark to get at his wallet.

Watching him move around the room in nothing but a pair of blue briefs, however, put her on information overload. She averted her gaze until he switched off the bathroom light.

Her discomfort increased when Micah threw himself on the bed next to her, softly whispering, "Night, Angel."

Though his use of the abbreviated name annoyed her, she didn't respond, merely stared into the dark, too aware of his closeness. Heat seemed to radiate from every pore of his body. She began sweating inside the wedding gown.

Which activated her imagination.

How could she help but envision the two of them in bed together under very different circumstances...his hands on her, not trying to force her or to drag her anywhere but to seduce her.

Her body responded as if Micah really were making love to her. Her breasts tightened, as did the pit of her stomach. Shifting, she tried to find some relief, but no matter how she changed her position, some part of her seemed to be touching some part of him.

This had to stop! Talk about losing control...

Angela locked her thighs together and forced herself to recount meetings she had scheduled. Thinking about business was a sure way to kill lusty fantasies.

Eventually the muggy, musty room cooled and she did, too. Thankfully. She sensed Micah relaxing, finally giving way to his exhaustion. His breathing deepened as he sank into oblivion.

And Angela knew that her chance had finally arrived. Now or never.

Pulse threading unevenly, she first tested the waters by repositioning herself closer to the edge of the bed to see if she would disturb him. Micah's breathing remained even through several squeaks. He was out for the count.

Oh, so carefully she slipped off the mattress, a single metallic protest following her.

Barefoot, she sidled to the chair where he'd thrown his jeans, all the while keeping an eye on the lump in the bed. Her flesh rippled when he stirred—but he quickly settled down. His wallet nearly jumped into her hand. She withdrew most of the cash, leaving him with pocket change and his credit cards. After stuffing the wad into the front of her corset, she slid the wallet back into his jeans, where her fingers came upon the car keys.

Her heart skipped a beat. She could take the Thunderbird and get to somewhere with a bus stop before he even knew it was missing. *But his car...* He was obviously fond of the old beater. Taking money she meant to return was one thing, but the other was out of the question. She was merely bending her ethics, not abandoning them.

On the way to the door she stopped to pick up her shoes by the bed and check Micah's breathing once more. Still deep and even. A sudden snore startled her and she feared he would wake himself. But he merely turned onto his stomach, his arm flopping over what was supposed to be her side of the bed. His hand landed close to her face.

Too close.

Heart thumping, she inched away, rose and tried to finesse the door. The sharp clicks of the lock sounded like gunshots. But Micah didn't so much as twitch and her pulse quickly settled. She opened the door and slid into the night.

Finally free, she stuffed her feet back into her shoes.

She should have taken the car keys, after all, she realized suddenly—she could have left them on the dash. Not only could she have grabbed the cell phone, but she could have taken Mariscano's phone book and the computer printout she hadn't yet had a look at.

Hesitating, she considered returning to the room for the keys, then thought better of it. Too risky. She had to get going, and fast.

Who knew how long Micah would be dead to the world?

A quick look down the road revealed another truck stop with half a dozen vehicles parked outside. Surely someone would let her hitch a ride to the nearest town. She'd invent a cover story as she went.

But she'd gotten only steps from the motel-room door before it crashed open behind her.

Almost tripping over her own feet, Angela whipped around. Her stomach knotted as she faced the angry man who filled the doorway. Bathed in moonlight, Micah's skin seemed to glow. And what a lot of it there was. Continuing to inch backward, she assessed the situation. Shoeless and dressed only in his briefs, the bounty hunter was powerless to stop her.

"Where do you think you're going?" he asked almost too calmly.

An adrenaline rush charged through her, and she took off, yelling over her shoulder, "Anywhere away from you!"

Her euphoria was cut short when she heard the *slap-slap* of bare feet hurtling after her across the parking lot.

Chapter Seven

Panicked, Angela ran blindly. She had to get away. She had to regain control of her life, such as it was. Continuing to be held in Micah Kaminsky's grasp was a bitter pill she couldn't choke down.

But no matter that she ran as fast as her legs could pump, he caught up to her even before she set foot off the property. She imagined his breath on her neck. And she felt his hand wrap around her upper arm.

"Not again!" she screeched, jarring to a halt.

Refusing to give up so easily, she turned, free arm swinging. Her fist connected with the side of his face and she stomped his bare toes.

Micah howled in pain and hopped on one leg. But while his grip loosened, he managed to hang on. Dredging up a self-defense move she'd learned in college, she was able to hook her foot behind his knee. Only when she pulled did she realize she'd gone wrong somewhere. He came toppling like a felled tree, all right, but she was directly in his path. He smacked into her and sent her flying.

"No-o-o!"

But shouting couldn't stop gravity. Down she went, Micah on top of her, crushing her into the asphalt.

Trapped beneath his weight, she could barely move. Or breathe. Forget freeing herself.

Panting, she glowered at him. "Get off me!"

He was in no hurry to obey. "You're the one who put me here."

"My mistake."

"Trying to run was your mistake."

"Not as far as I'm concerned."

Starting to get claustrophobic under him, she gave moving him herself the college try. But going at him with hands and hips didn't so much as budge him.

"Not bad." His murmured response made it sound as if he'd enjoyed the experience. "Feel free to try that again."

Angela bit back an expletive and shoved again. A *r-r-rip* of material was her only reward.

"How far did you think you'd get without money?" Micah asked.

That threw her. The wad of cash suddenly itched where she'd wedged it in the corset.

She managed to force out "Far enough. C'mon, Kaminsky. You're crushing me."

"Micah," he corrected her. "And being crushed a little is the least you deserve. But I'll make nice if you promise not to try to run again."

"I don't lie well."

"I could probably fall asleep right here."

Angela clenched her jaw. He'd probably do it, too, unless he got what he wanted. Considering the difficulty she had breathing now, she'd probably be asphyxiated in no time.

"All right. I won't try to run again...*tonight.*"

"I guess that'll have to do."

His weight lifted, yet he didn't so much as offer her

a hand as he stood. Filled with disappointment at her failure, furious with herself for not taking the car keys after all, Angela awkwardly clambered to her feet. Micah didn't take his eyes off her. And his fingers manacled her wrist in a velvety trap that wrenched a response from her that she didn't want to acknowledge. She would *not* be attracted to this man anymore. That had been her problem from the first.

He started back across the parking lot, his pulling on her adding insult to injury. She jerked her arm, hoping to free it; his came, too.

Purposely staying a step behind him, she said, "Treating me like a child isn't necessary."

"I beg to differ."

"I gave you my word."

"The word of a Dragonlady."

"Stop calling me that!"

"Then stop acting like one. *Angel.*"

"I *hate* that."

"Make up your mind."

Meaning he was determined to call her one wretched name or the other?

As he towed her toward the motel, a pair of senior citizens exited the office. Clutching their room key, the man practically danced along the sidewalk, his hand on his companion's behind. The woman giggled like a schoolgirl. Catching sight of her and Micah, they stopped as one, eyes wide, and blocked the way.

"Look, sugar," the man said. "Newlyweds." He beamed. "Congratulations."

"Thank you," Micah returned sociably...as if he weren't prancing around nearly naked.

The woman gave him an appreciative once-over. Angela used the distraction to work on prying his fingers from around her wrist.

The woman clucked at her. "Don't worry, dear. No matter what your mother told you, the physical aspects of being married are quite enjoyable. Nothing to run away from."

The kindly lecture making her want to sink right into the ground, Angela stared at the pavement beneath her feet. "I'll keep that in mind."

She had to do something about the damn gown. Surely she could find a way to alter it so she wouldn't be mistaken for a newlywed again.

"Good luck," the man said, scurrying his sweetie off to their room.

"Don't worry, Angel," Micah said, purposely speaking loudly enough for them to hear. "I'll make this a night you'll never forget."

"I *do* have a long memory," she threatened in return.

She ought to have told the couple what was really going on. But either they would have called the authorities or tried to stop Micah themselves. The first would have meant trading one jailer for another. As for the second—who knew what the bounty hunter might have done to physically overpower the poor elderly couple?

Even as she thought it, Angela knew she was being unfair. Micah hadn't actually done a thing to hurt her...though his frame of mind might have shifted now.

Once in the room, he forced her onto the bed, which squeaked and squealed until she settled down. Then he found his jeans and, shoving his hand into the pocket, pulled out his wallet. He balanced it in his hand for a moment before setting it down and digging out the car keys. Leaving the pants on the chair, he headed for the door, apparently unconcerned about his state of undress.

Angela couldn't stop herself. "What are you doing?"

"I have a surprise. Don't try to leave before I can give it to you."

If that doesn't have an ominous ring...

She glared him out of the room. Surprise, indeed. Nothing he could do would throw her after what she'd been through in less than twenty-four hours. Rather than playing guessing games, she needed to formulate Plan B.

But Micah didn't even give her enough time to get started. He was back in a flash, hiding something behind his back. She thoroughly distrusted his benign smile as he planted himself at the side of the bed.

"What?"

"I promised you a surprise. Hold out your hand."

She narrowed her gaze. "I don't think so."

Before she knew what was happening, he took hold of her right hand anyway and placed something cold and hard around her wrist.

"Hey!"

Click.

Shocked at being handcuffed, she scowled at him, not realizing exactly what he was about until he pulled it up to the headboard. She tried to stop him, whipping up her other arm, and for her trouble, played right into his plan. He cuffed her other wrist.

Handcuffed to the headboard! How dare he!

For a moment she was speechless. No one had ever treated her so callously. But Angela wasn't one to let things go without a protest.

"What if I have to go to the bathroom in the middle of the night?" she demanded, then was sorry she had found her voice.

His smirk of satisfaction grated on her nerves.

"Wake me. Maybe I'll be able to find the right key."

Furious, she tugged at the headboard, willing it to fall apart. But it proved more solidly built than the rest of the creaky motel.

"*Now* maybe I can get some sleep," he said, throwing himself down next to her.

Now?

"You weren't sleeping before?"

"Knowing you were up to something? Not hardly. Where'd you hide the cash?"

"Excuse me?"

"You know—the green stuff you stole from my wallet."

"I planned to pay back every penny."

"Sure you did. Where is it?"

He didn't believe her. He not only thought she was a liar, but a thief, as well.

Micah shifted and straddled her. Bringing his face close to hers, he softly asked, "Where, Angel?"

Fearing he would dream up further degradations by searching her if she didn't confess, Angela figured giving it up was the wisest course.

"Undo these handcuffs and I'll get the money for you."

He laughed softly and shook his head. "Don't think so. Not when I finally have you where I want you."

His wording gave her a start. What exactly did he mean? Aware that she was vulnerable, that he could do anything to her and she couldn't stop him, Angela felt an unfamiliar anxiety creep through her. Her stomach knotted and her mouth went so dry that she could hardly speak.

"In front."

"You're wearing a garter?"

She shook her head once and closed her eyes so she didn't have to look into his face. "The bodice."

"You won't mind if I relieve you of what's mine."

Her whole body stiff with tension, she gritted her teeth against the imagined ordeal.

Micah lifted his weight from her chest, his thighs remaining around her hips. Then his fingers lightly dipped into the hollow between her breasts. Her flesh pebbled and she sucked in her breath, waiting to see what he would do.

The crackle of paper told her he'd found the bills. Grasping the money, he freed it from her corset...

...Then rolled back to his side, the springs protesting with a series of squeaks.

That was it?

Angela opened one eye to see him *counting the money!* He didn't even trust her to return it all. Anger sputtered through her lips as she finally released her breath.

"Something wrong?" he asked with a wide-eyed expression of the completely innocent.

She refused to dignify his question with an answer. He shrugged and replaced the bills in his wallet, then flipped off the room light.

Within seconds he fell back into bed with a groan.

Within minutes he was snoring.

And Angela was left wide awake with her disappointment and mortification.

Handcuffed like a common criminal—this was beyond bearing. She'd wanted only to be free of him, to take her life back, but at every turn he took the upper hand.

And he hadn't done it alone, Angela admitted ruefully.

She couldn't forget the part she'd played at the truck stop. She'd been so wrapped up in their game of one-upmanship that she hadn't even tried to get away. Well, no more. Finally her head was on straight, and when she put her mind to it, nothing could stop her from getting what she wanted. From coming out on top. From being number one.

Starting now, she'd let nothing distract her.

Especially not Micah Kaminsky.

She spent awhile sorting through and discarding various options—ways of overcoming Micah's sheer superior strength. Her strength lay in her intelligence.

Think. Concentrate.

One moment her mind was blank. The next, a workable idea came to her, though she was chagrined at having to take advantage of the wedding gown after wanting to be free of it. The more she thought about it, the more the notion appealed to her, until she finally embraced it despite the negatives. Micah wouldn't give her up without a fight. She would choose her champion carefully.

Though she'd never approved of violence, these were desperate times....

That settled, Angela figured she'd better concentrate on getting some sleep. She needed all her resources if she was going to succeed.

But try as she might, she couldn't ignore the warm body stretched out alongside her. Every time she tried, the kiss replayed itself in her mind, and she wondered what it would have been like had it been for real.

And when he rolled onto his side, his arm sliding across her waist, she wondered what it would be like to be held in Micah's arms voluntarily.

How ridiculous. The bounty hunter was all wrong for her—not that he was interested, anyway—and if her plan went according to schedule, she would be free of him at last. And then she'd never have to see him again, voluntarily or otherwise. He would be out of her life for good.

A small ache that she could never satisfy...that went beyond the physical...began creeping through her.

She'd get him for that, too.

THE NEXT MORNING BEGAN dismally, her plan off schedule from the start. At dawn, Micah left her trapped in the room while he fetched a minimalist breakfast. She consumed doughnuts and coffee with one hand, while the other remained cuffed and secured to the headboard.

"Afraid you can't even control me while you're awake?" she asked, setting her paper coffee cup down on the chair he'd been so accommodating to provide.

Swallowing the last of what had to be his fifth doughnut, he said, "I'm choosing to err on the side of caution."

He was erring, big time. Angela was counting the moments.

That he didn't keep her handcuffed inside the car once they got on the road took her by surprise. That and his not playing twenty questions as they cruised west toward the Minnesota border. He knew enough about her, anyway. And she knew so little about him. Time to change that. Maybe he'd even let down his guard.

"So, how old were you when you decided you wanted to be a bounty hunter?"

Sunglasses masking his gaze once more, he glanced at her. "Actually, that was never a goal of mine."

"What was?"

"Staying out of jail, mostly."

Struck by the odd answer, Angela frowned. She supposed his being from the inner city meant he'd had to become a member of a gang to survive. Maybe that's where he'd learned to derail alarm systems and such. But no matter his background, surely he'd had dreams of some sort.

"That's the first time I've heard of 'staying out of jail' as being someone's goal in life."

"Funny, I thought we had that in common."

The reminder put her back up. "We don't have anything in common."

"I know. You're a lady and I'm what? Common? A boor?"

She'd never said that. "Rough around the edges."

"A nice way of putting it."

"At least I'm honest."

"Are you? About everything?"

She lifted her chin. "Of course."

"I'm surprised no one's nominated you for sainthood."

If he was trying to irritate her, he was doing a fair job. Under other circumstances, he might have been able to get her going. But Angela kept her plan in mind, and, therefore, her temper under control.

"You're getting off track." Purposely, no doubt, so he wouldn't have to open up. "We were talking about *you*," she reminded him. "If I'm forced to be in your company, I should at least know something about you more than name, rank and serial number." Actually, she didn't even know that much. "So what about your family? You have a family, right? Or did you pop out of a pod?"

"Now I'm a pod person?" He snorted. "How Mom would have liked your sense of humor."

"Would have?"

"Would have," he echoed soberly.

"I'm sorry."

"Not as much as I am."

At least she had her parents. *Parent*, she corrected herself, since her father didn't count. So maybe she and Micah did have something in common—having both lost someone they loved, if in different ways.

"What about the rest of your family?"

"Pop's partial to sweet, softhearted women with forgiving natures," Micah said. "Though he probably would appreciate your...uh, spirit...once he got used to you. My younger brother, Harry, loves any woman who's smart and attractive. And our little sister, Rona, would say that I deserved you."

Deserved her?

That sounding far too personal, she said, "The question wasn't about me."

"I thought everything was about you."

Stung into silence, Angela fumed. Micah made her sound selfish and spoiled, while she was neither. She'd never had the time or interest to be self-indulgent. She worked hard, always had...and she'd always kept her family's welfare uppermost in mind.

Without her own hand guiding the business, they would have been comfortable. She had no doubts her mother would have seen to that even if the poor woman had had to work herself into the ground. Angela had never played modest about being the one who had propelled Here Comes the Bride into growing and diversifying, becoming a viable company rather than a small business. But she hadn't worked so hard for herself alone.

If Micah believed she had, he didn't know her half as well as he thought he did.

Plan B nudged to be liberated.

"I need to make a pit stop," she announced.

"Soon," he promised.

But rather than taking an exit to a truck stop or town, he pulled off at a state rest stop. Tourists—mostly families with kids—filled the building that boasted maps as well as drinking fountains and rest rooms. No one she could single out here. Several transport trucks sat in the separate parking lot on the other side of the building, but the drivers remained near their vehicles.

Back on the road, she waited a while before complaining, "I'm starving. Those doughnuts don't last forever."

"Check the backseat. You'll find some sandwiches in an insulated bag."

Headed off again.

Every bite of the sandwich nearly choked her with frustration.

Angela was wound up tight by the time they crossed the Mississippi River into Minnesota. Micah finally picked up speed as did the drivers around them. A Jeep came darting out of nowhere, nearly cutting them off before dropping back. As she saw it, she realized they were hurtling away from civilization, and her chances for escape were dwindling.

"This seat is getting to me," she complained as they paralleled the river. "I need to get out of the car and stretch my back."

"If we keep stopping, we'll never get to Nevada. Though I suppose that's the idea."

"Sorry I'm not accustomed to being trapped in a moving vehicle for hours at a time."

"Get used to it."

As heartless as he sounded, Micah took the turnoff to

the state park facing the river. This time, however, he avoided the information center and the few passenger vehicles parked in the lot. Angela noted they were on a bluff overlooking a section of the Mississippi's lock and dam system. He pulled in to a slot facing the mighty river.

She slid out of the Thunderbird and took note of two semis parked at the far end of the lot. The drivers were nowhere to be seen. No doubt they were either inside the information center or getting some shut-eye.

Her only hope was to stall.

Gazing longingly at the concrete promenade running along the river, she sighed. "A walk would do me wonders."

The mirrored sunglasses winked at her where the sun struck them. Her paranoia was growing in leaps and bounds, because she swore Micah could not only sense her tension, but could read her mind as to what she was plotting.

Yet, finally, he agreed. "Five minutes. And don't—"

"Try anything. Right."

After preceding him down the few steps to the walkway, she glanced back toward the road exiting from the highway. Though it was clear now, two vehicles had arrived after them. A minivan near the information building released several kids with pent-up energy. She could hear their screams as they ran, one bumping into the other. And a tan four-by-four had stopped in the shade of a big maple tree.

"I thought you wanted to walk."

His breath fluttered the hair around her face...and with it Angela's insides. Micah was practically standing on top of her. Too aware of him for her own comfort, she didn't need further encouragement to move off.

"I was just getting my bearings." She scanned the river, where a barge was trapped in the system, waiting for the water to rise so it could move upstream. "Amazing how even the mightiest river can be harnessed."

"Using the correct techniques, anything can be controlled."

Disliking the intimate tone of his voice—not to mention the underlying meaning—she swept ahead, murmuring, "I wouldn't be so sure of myself if I were you."

Perched on a bench, an elderly man stared out at the activity on the water. From the opposite direction a harried-looking woman passed them pushing a stroller with one hand—the baby inside was screaming—and hanging on to an unruly toddler with the other. A teenaged couple huddled together in the shelter of a tree, the girl giggling softly as her boyfriend whispered in her ear.

Despite herself, Angela was enjoying the walk with Micah. For once he didn't press her buttons, merely kept her company. And nature had a way of soothing her anxiety, anyway. The sun. The breeze. Even the river, though its progress was artificially controlled in this area. She tuned in to the water's rush over the dam and absently swatted a mosquito that was lunching on her arm.

The place was loaded with bloodthirsty insects.

Even so, reality intruded all too soon when Micah said, "Your five minutes are up."

Reminding her she was his prisoner. "So they are."

Not letting her disappointment get to her, Angela obediently turned back, her gaze sweeping the parking lot. Her spirits were buoyed by an eighteen-wheeler crawling into a parking slot.

Knowing she had to stall a bit, Angela made a show

of stopping and stretching, rotating her shoulders and neck. "Oh, yeah, that's feeling a lot better."

"Good." As if he suspected something, Micah suddenly grew impatient. "Then we can get going."

"We certainly can."

Ascending the half-dozen steps to the parking lot, she eyed the trucker climbing down from his cab. The situation was better than she'd hoped for. The burly, middle-aged man was big enough to dwarf Micah. Pacing her stride so they would pass him as he lumbered over to the information center, Angela controlled her growing excitement.

And ignored the regret brushing her deep inside.

Several yards from the trucker, she found the tear in her sleeve, a result of her roll on the pavement with Micah the night before. She stuck her fingers through the hole in the delicate material.

"Look at this, Micah! You ruined it!"

Micah's shaded gaze met hers. "So?"

"You don't even care about my wedding gown?" she cried loudly, getting the trucker's full attention. "I should have listened to Mother when she warned me about you."

"*Angel...*"

"Don't *Angel* me! A wedding license doesn't give you permission to be a brute!"

"Stop it, right now," he ordered through clenched teeth.

He wrapped his fingers around her upper arm even as the trucker was about to pass them.

"Ouch! That's where you bruised me before." She stopped dead and gave the stranger an embarrassed expression before averting her gaze. "This is a big mistake, Micah. I don't want to be with you anymore."

"I don't care what you want."

"Well, I care," the trucker said, stopping also. "The little lady don't want to go with you no more, she don't have to."

"Stay out of this."

"Yes, please," Angela said, trying her best to sound sincere. "I wouldn't want you to get hurt. You don't know what he's like when he's riled."

"I ain't afraid of the likes of him, ma'am." The burly man's supportive gaze swept over her. Then his eyes widened and his forehead furrowed. "Hey, what'd you do to your wife's arm to make her bleed like that?"

Bleed?

Angela quickly glanced down and saw a dried trickle of red trailing from her forearm to her wrist. The mosquito. She gasped and pretended to go all woozy.

And Micah made the mistake of shaking her. "Let's go!" Then tried forcing her.

"No, *you* go!" the trucker said, grabbing the front of Micah's T-shirt and pulling him a little off balance.

His expression both surprised and angry, Micah released her. "This isn't your business, buddy."

"I'm makin' it my business. You hightail it outta here and I'll see to the little lady."

"See to yourself." Micah shoved at the stranger. "She's *my* bride."

Angela was struck by the possessive tone that sounded far too real, and her pulse skittered as the trucker's face twisted with ire.

"Your bride ain't interested."

His free arm pulled back. He swung, his hamlike fist going directly for Micah's face.

Cringing, she experienced a moment's regret.

Wasted energy.

Micah ducked out of the way, threw up his arm to break the other man's hold and landed a hard punch directly in the middle of the broad solar plexus.

The trucker caved in with a soft "Oof!"

And Micah simply grabbed Angela's wrist and dragged her. Fighting was useless.

"I'm sorry!" she yelled to the stranger, who was bent forward, clutching his gut.

"I'll get you help!" he promised, staggering back to his rig.

Several other people exiting the information center stopped at their vehicles as Micah shoved her into the Thunderbird. Two men who'd parked the tan four-by-four under the tree got out and watched. No additional offer of assistance came her way, however, convincing Angela that she was, for some unknown reason, cursed.

Doomed to be Micah Kaminsky's captive until the end of time.

Or until they reached Nevada.

Whichever came first.

"WE SHOULDA STEPPED IN," one man said as they clambered back into the rental Jeep.

His fair-haired companion gave him a withering look. "With all these witnesses?"

He fastened his seat belt as one of the nosy tourists approached the trucker. The burly man was fishing for something in his cab.

"She was trying to get rid of the wild card. These yokels woulda applauded us."

"And remembered what we looked like."

He didn't take his eyes off the trucker. Damn! The buffoon was on the CB.

"Yeah, you got a point," the dark-haired man said.

''Now that we're on their trail, we just gotta wait for the right opportunity. We'll get 'em.''

They certainly would....

''If the cops don't catch up to them first.''

Chapter Eight

"I figured we were done with all this game playing," Micah said as soon as they were back on the road and he was certain no eighteen-wheeler was bearing down on them.

"What you're doing to me is no game."

"You're right, Angela. Your situation is serious."

And far more complex than he'd been led to believe. He checked his rear mirror again. All clear. For now. That trucker wasn't going to let this alone, not after promising Angela that he'd get her help. Micah knew this in his gut. He expected to see a column of state police vehicles overtaking them at any moment.

Maybe that would be the best solution for her, no matter what she believed.

As for him...claustrophobia was already threatening to choke him...he could sense those familiar prison walls closing in.

"Micah..."

Angela startled him from the nightmare into paying attention to his driving. "Yeah?"

"Why are you so determined to hand me over to the authorities when I'm perfectly willing not only to match but to exceed the reward you'll get for bringing me in?"

He unclenched his hands, clammy with anticipation and dread. "I never said I was doing this for money."

"Next you'll be telling me you're only interested in seeing justice done."

"Is that so unbelievable—that *my kind* respects the law?"

Her passing judgment on him without knowing anything about what he'd done with his life continued to rankle.

"I saw proof of how much you respect the law when you broke into Mariscano's house."

He couldn't believe it. "Getting inside was *your* idea. I went along with it to get you off my back," he rationalized. Even knowing the penalty if they'd been caught. "And—"

"And you disarmed a sophisticated security system. I wonder where you developed that kind of talent."

"Maybe in my former life as a burglar," he said acidly.

"Former?"

Meaning she thought that's what he did for a living now?

Micah was ready to strangle her. Again. No woman had ever been able to get to him the way Angela did. She got under his skin in the worst way.

In the most frustrating way.

He should have left her to the trucker. Then they'd both be happy. Sighing, Micah knew that was a lie, at least for him. He warned himself not to get involved. The moment Angela was out of sight, he'd start worrying about her.

He hadn't worried about a woman in more years than he cared to count. Why this one?

"Look, I'm ready to make a deal," he said, not seeing

any other way. "No more games. What would it take to get you to agree?"

"You're ready to let me go?"

"Other than that."

"Don't take me back to Nevada."

"That's the same thing and you know it."

"All right." Desperation edged her voice. "When we get there, don't turn me over to the authorities. If I don't find out who set me up, no one will."

He hesitated, as if thinking it over. "Agreed."

He felt her narrowed gaze on him when she echoed, "Agreed?"

"My word as a...rough-around-the-edges man."

She didn't even crack a smile. "I don't understand. Wasn't the whole idea to—"

"Get you back to Nevada. I'll deliver you directly to your doorstep."

Her voice was filled with distrust when she said, "After calling the authorities, right?"

"No call to the authorities. Pinkie swear." He crooked and held out his little finger, which she ignored, maybe because he hadn't sworn that he wouldn't call anyone at all. "So what do you say? Do we have a deal?"

He uncurled the rest of his fingers and waited.

"I haven't had a better offer lately." She slipped her hand into his. "Deal."

Most women had a soft shake that he loathed, as if they were trying to prove how delicate—feminine?—they were. Angela clasping his hand as if she meant it both impressed and affected him. In her handshake, he recognized not only her strength—which he found sexy if not delicately feminine—but her transfer of trust.

Why? He couldn't figure it. She held on to that trust

the way some women held on to their virginity. She withheld it from her old man because of something he'd done decades ago that had nothing to do with her. That she'd given it to *him,* a near stranger, was downright puzzling.

Either that or she didn't mean a word of this deal, and he was a bigger fool than he wanted to admit.

"And I promise I'll make it up to you," Angela was saying. "Monetarily, I mean."

Micah removed his hand from hers and clenched his jaw so he wouldn't say something he couldn't take back.

Realizing she'd been holding his attention a bit too closely, he automatically checked all his mirrors. A tan recreational vehicle kept its distance directly behind him, but on his right he caught the reflection of a transport truck coming up fast. He started until he remembered the guy he'd decked had been driving a semi with a yellow cab. This one was shiny red.

He relaxed and let his mind drift back to Angela and the offending offer.

Her phobia about money probably stemmed from what she saw as her father's abandonment. To having everything and then nothing, at least in her mind. Micah was pretty sure she appreciated what she did have in her mother and siblings, but she seemed to measure the outside world—and therefore him—in monetary terms. Natural, he expected, considering her circumstances.

Because he figured Angela was being sincere and offering him what she thought he wanted, Micah decided his best bet was to not say anything to her on the subject at all.

ASSUMING MICAH WOULD HOLD up his end of the bargain was a stretch for Angela, and yet she imagined he might come through for her. She wanted to believe it.

Wanted to believe in him.

Worrying at the tear in her sleeve, she accidentally made the hole bigger, then decided to finish the job in hopes of feeling a bit more comfortable. She purposely ripped at the material, until all that was left was a cap to cover her shoulder.

"It was looking pretty shabby," she said, knowing she had Micah's attention. "Now I have to figure out how to make the other one match."

He fished something from one of his vest pockets. "Use this."

The object she took from him proved to be a knife barely large enough to cradle in the curve of her palm. Of solid ebony on one side, the handle was inlaid with varicolored hardwood on the other.

"This is a beautiful piece of work."

"Pop gave it to me."

Unable to miss the depth of emotion in Micah's voice, Angela ran her finger along the marquetry. "You must trust me if you're letting me use it."

"Let's say I don't think you have it in you to *literally* go out for someone's blood. Not even mine."

And that's not what she'd meant. He obviously treasured the present from his father and trusted her to treat it with the proper care.

She slipped the three-inch blade from its sheath and made quick work of the second sleeve, then sliced through the threads that attached the silk roses to her bodice. Only after she'd removed the bunch and chucked it to the backseat did she realize her neckline was even lower than before. From her point of view, it looked as if she would spill out of the dress if she so much as leaned too far forward. She fought the urge to grab the material and tug it up toward her chin.

Without taking his eyes off the road, Micah held out his hand. So much for his trusting her. She snapped the knife shut and dropped it into his palm.

Not much else she could do to the dress to make herself comfortable, anyway. If only she could rid herself of the corset, which had become an object of torture. She wanted in the worst way to be free of the straitjacket feeling that threatened to cut off her air supply. Permanently.

"You know, we really need to stop somewhere so I can get a change of clothing."

"You won't be stuck in that thing much longer."

"Hah! My best guess is that we have approximately two thousand miles to go, a day and a half of straight, no-sleep driving...and we know that's not going to happen unless you trade off with me."

"Let *you* drive?"

Disliking his incredulous tone, she informed him, "I do have a license...though not on me, of course."

"But the *Thunderbird?*"

He acted as if the old bucket of bolts were sacred. Men and their attachments to rusting hunks of metal!

She should have saved her breath. No way would Micah let her behind the wheel of his precious car. With only him driving, Angela figured she'd be spending at least three more days in Micah's company, a fact that didn't bother her as it should. As it had before...

Before what?

Barely an hour ago she'd set Micah up to take a fall. She'd been willing to see him sprawled across the pavement, nose bloodied—if not worse—so she could get away. She couldn't explain her own change of heart, not when she didn't understand it herself.

Her only excuse was that stress had to be warping her judgment. "So what about the clothes?" she asked, returning to her original point.

"I always carry a spare in the trunk," he offered. "Next pit stop—"

"Oh, that'll do swell. Now you want me to wear rubber. A little too kinky for me, even if I do like *spankings* and all," she said, reminding him of his bawdy comments to the ladies at the gas station.

"Actually, I was thinking of denim."

"You won't mind if I cut several inches off the pant legs, will you? Or perhaps I should make do with that T-shirt you offered me last night. T-shirt dresses are always in fashion, you know," she said sarcastically. Though the idea didn't sound too bad, comfortwise, she still had some pride in her appearance. She refused to consider how the shredded gown looked. "And you undoubtedly have a piece of rope in the trunk that I can use as a makeshift belt."

"I'm sure I do," he said amiably. "And if you get chilly at night, I have a long-sleeved flannel shirt you can throw over it."

"Plaid, I assume?"

"It's even your colors—red and black."

"With socks to match?"

"Sorry. I don't color coordinate my—"

"Get real!" Angela snapped, having no clue whether or not he was serious. "I'm not prancing around like an idiot in your clothes."

"You'd be a more comfortable idiot."

"I'd be a happy idiot if we stopped somewhere so I could buy a few things that fit me properly."

"With what? You don't have any money, remember."

"Not since you retrieved it." She swallowed hard at the memory of his fingers fishing around beneath the corset. "So float me a loan and I'll pay back—"

"Every penny?"

"And make up your mind before we pass Rochester." She'd already seen signs announcing the exits were coming up in the next several miles. "It isn't Minneapolis, but surely they have a shopping center or two. Heck, I'll do a jig for an outfit from some discount place."

"Is that a promise?"

"You want me to put it in writing? I'll sign it in blood if you insist."

"All right, all right. But don't open a vein yet. You'll ruin your new outfit."

She gaped. "Really? You mean it?" She'd actually talked him into something?

"Whatever you can buy for a double sawbuck."

"Twenty dollars?" Worrying that he might withdraw the offer if she sounded ungrateful, she quickly finished, "Will do me fine."

Even though she normally paid more than that just for her underwear, she'd manage to make do or her name wasn't Angela Dragon.

"In the meantime," she went on, "where's that file of Mariscano's you printed out?" His vest was nowhere in sight. "About time we took a good look, don't you think?"

"It's in the trunk. I'll fish it out when we stop."

For a woman who expected instant results when she wanted something, Angela decided she was becoming far too well acquainted with the virtue of patience.

MICAH FIGURED he was being paranoid, but he wasn't crazy about the red-cabbed truck exiting behind them.

Nor about its turning in the same direction and following them the half mile to the busy suburban intersection flanked by businesses. The tension didn't flow out of him until the rig slowed and turned in at a gas station advertising diesel fuel. Relieved, Micah headed for the Target sign at the end of the strip mall on the other side of the road.

"Ready to do that jig?"

"Once I'm wearing something I can move in."

"Seems to me you've been moving pretty well."

"Just think of what I can do in real clothes."

Micah grinned. Although as feisty as always, Angela sounded as if she was in a better mood than he'd experienced since nabbing her. She almost sounded happy. He could get used to the change.

He could get used to her.

That thought was wiped clear out of his mind, however, when he crossed the road and saw the state police car cruising the parking lot. Why? Normally, private security forces would be on patrol. His antennae out, he avoided the official vehicle, purposely circling a row of cars.

"What are you doing? You keep passing up empty spots."

"Checking things out."

Since the patrol car seemed to have disappeared, Micah parked. But when he left the Thunderbird, caution remained foremost in his mind. That Angela was practically doing that jig down the aisle alarmed him.

"Wait up."

"I can't wait any longer." She stepped into the road fronting the store. "*You* hurry!"

She was moving fast. And from the corner of his eye

he saw a blur moving even faster—a vehicle heading straight toward her.

"Angela!" He started running as he yelled, "Get out of the way!"

She glanced over her shoulder, then ducked to the side as a tan Jeep nearly sideswiped her.

"Idiot!" she yelled. "Where'd you get your driver's license?"

The Jeep squealed to a stop and began to back up.

People were stopping to watch.

And the state police car was heading their way.

Not about to wait for introductions, Micah grabbed Angela's wrist and jerked her back the way they'd come.

"Hey, what do you think you're doing?"

"Saving your butt."

"From who?"

"We could wait to find out if you don't mind talking to the state police."

"My new clothes!" she wailed while putting on some speed. "I'm never going to get out of this cursed gown."

A glance back assured Micah he'd done the right thing. The driver of the Jeep had his window rolled down, and a state trooper was talking to the guy but looking their way. The cop straightened, the sun's reflection winking off his sunglasses, and said something over his shoulder to his partner in the squad. He never averted his gaze.

A bad feeling in his gut, Micah started the Thunderbird and tried to maintain an aura of calm as he drove down the aisle and turned back onto the road. The whole time he kept aware of what was going on in front of the store. The trooper got on the horn while the Jeep drove off.

Had the trucker he'd decked made an official complaint about him?

He imagined an APB with his description....

By the time they approached the expressway, his palms were damp and nervous perspiration coated his entire body. Seemingly unaware of how close a call they'd had, Angela mourned the loss of the new clothing.

"I can't believe this...trapped in a wedding gown! I was close...so close...I can almost feel those new clothes on my body. Why did you have to drag me off because some idiot was speeding through a parking lot? *He* was the one in the wrong."

"But he wasn't the one the trooper was interested in," Micah said. "He was fixated on us."

"Of course he was. We were running, for heaven's sake. No doubt he imagined we had reason to get out and fast." She paused for a breath before asking, "You don't have any outstanding warrants or anything?"

"I can always count on you to assume the best about me." Exasperated with her one track mind when it came to him personally, he checked his mirrors for any sign of the state troopers following. "No doubt you'd get a bang seeing me behind bars."

No state patrol car, but a semi was directly behind them. One with a red cab. Surely not the *same* truck.

He was so intent on the unexpected vision that he barely heard Angela's "Not anymore."

"What?"

"I did want to see you behind bars at first," she admitted. "Either that or roasting over hot coals."

She was grinning at him, and her eyes were sparkling, making him almost forget about the semi. Almost.

Speeding up, he checked the rearview mirror. The

other driver must have stepped on it also, since the distance between him and the red cab stayed the same. If the guy were just in a hurry, surely he would go around...

"Did you get a good look at the semi that followed us off the interstate before?"

"I saw it, sure," she said, her tone questioning.

"Check out the one behind us. Could that be the same truck?"

"Got me. But there's another eighteen-wheeler coming up on the right."

She wasn't taking him seriously. Micah wasn't taking himself seriously...until he glanced in the passenger side mirror and noted the color of the cab.

Bright yellow.

"Uh-oh."

A glance in his own side mirror revealed a third truck with a blue cab coming up on him even faster.

"What the..."

"Micah, slow down!"

His gaze flew to the front windshield at the same time his foot lifted from the accelerator. They were bearing down on a fourth semi. He started to switch lanes...until the truck ahead swerved in front of him.

"What's going on?" Angela asked with a frightened gasp.

"I'm getting a bad feeling about this," he muttered.

Which got even worse when he realized yet another truck ahead was slowing, as if getting into a predetermined position. Though he again tried to make a break, the driver cut him off. Then Micah knew for certain. Angela's champion hadn't used the CB to alert the authorities. He'd called on men who formed a much closer bond, who looked out for each other on the road.

Within seconds they formed a convoy. Half a dozen semis and the Thunderbird.

"We're surrounded."

"What's going on?" Angela asked, whipping around in her seat to get a better look.

"I'd say you're getting that help you were wanting so badly earlier."

The trucks were slowing down and he could do nothing but follow suit. He had no choice. No out unless he wanted to take a serious chance with their lives. The worst the truckers would do would be to liberate Angela, beat him to a pulp and leave him for dead.

Micah guessed that was an improvement over an almost guaranteed seventy-mile-an-hour wreck.

Allowing the T-bird to be forced off the road at the next turnoff, he realized they were stopping at a truck weighing station. No exit to Eden, that was for certain. No witnesses. No one to turn to for succor.

They were trapped. *He* was trapped.

And Angela was probably eating this up.

But when he cut the engine and faced her, she didn't seem to be gloating. A frown creased her forehead as she glanced out the front windshield. The drivers were climbing down from their cabs and she actually seemed to be worried.

At least, he hoped so.

"Uh-oh, I think you'd better leave this one to me," she said.

Micah grimaced. "You want to close the lid on my coffin personally?"

"Don't be ridiculous." Her almond eyes narrowed on him. "I got you into this mess. I'll get you out."

Finding that one hard to swallow, considering he didn't trust her as far as he could throw her, Micah pictured himself lying facedown on the asphalt and her driving off in the Thunderbird, one hand on the wheel, the other waving his wallet at him.

But a half-dozen burly men were surrounding the car. He didn't have time to play devil's advocate with her. Besides, fool that he was, he wanted to believe she wouldn't set him up again.

With a resigned groan, he muttered, "My life is in your hands." For however long he still had it.

Getting out of the car, he experienced major claustrophobia when the two youngest and healthiest-looking drivers immediately closed in on him. They formed a human sandwich—with him feeling exactly like the meat in the middle.

The trucker he'd decked stepped forward, his concerned gaze hovering on Angela as if he were trying to make certain she was still in one piece. "Are you all right, little lady?"

"I'm fine."

"And you're gonna stay that way. When Billy Bob Johnson makes a promise, he comes through."

Angela donned the most grateful, most embarrassed, most conciliatory expression Micah had ever seen.

"I can't thank you enough," she cooed, batting her eyes as if it came naturally to her.

And that after denying eye-batting was her style.

"You boys are real honest-to-goodness heroes."

"Our mamas raised us to take care of our women," an older driver said. "Not like some."

He turned agate eyes on Micah, who was trying to decide if he'd actually said *some*…or *scum*. And his gut tightened as he figured Angela was going to reclaim her freedom at his expense.

What else should he have expected?

Angela couldn't believe the mess she'd gotten them in, and this after she'd finally come to terms with Micah. Good thing she was expert at backpedaling. She made eye contact with her chief rescuer.

"I really do appreciate your concern and the fact that you acted when you thought I was in trouble, Billy Bob, but...and this is the thing...it's all *my* fault...what happened at the state park, I mean."

Billy Bob shook his head. "Men like him always make women think they're in the wrong when they get busted up." His gaze sweeping her tattered clothing, he shook his head. "Just look at what's left of that wedding gown of yours. And your hair...tch, tch, tch."

Her hand flew to her head and the bald spot she quickly covered by combing her hair with her fingers. "No, really. I was angry with Micah for not trusting me. Just because my old boyfriend wanted me back didn't mean I was going to go with him."

"She was trying to teach me a lesson."

She gave Micah a melting look despite the intensity of his gaze at her. Despite the fact that she wanted to scream at him to keep his mouth shut for once and let her handle things. Anxious that he'd spoil her strategy by saying something he shouldn't, she quickly continued.

"I knew I was being childish when Micah hauled off on you. A mistake. *My* mistake." Gazing around at her heroes—she'd really meant that part—she said, "I never should have involved anyone else."

"What about his hurting you?"

"An exaggeration," she admitted. "I was so angry I wasn't thinking straight. I can't tell you how sorry I am that you went to all this trouble for nothing." She glanced from one suspicious expression to another. "Everything is fine, I promise. Tell me how I can make it up to you guys.''

"I don't know..."

"Please. If anyone got hurt or in trouble with the *law* because of me—'' she emphasized the second to make them think twice before getting in deeper ''—I would never forgive myself.''

"You're sure you're okay?'' one of Micah's body-guards asked.

"Positive. Absolutely.''

Her smile seemed to melt any belligerence the men had left against Micah. One of them started back for his truck.

"Hey, the lady has spoken," he said. "Let's leave them be.''

Grumblings were followed by agreement and the res-cue party broke up. The men headed for their rigs, only Billy Bob still seeming reluctant to leave.

"Thanks again," she said. "And I'm sorry Micah punched you before." She couldn't help herself. "If it would make you feel better, you could return the favor.''

He gave Micah a searing look that told her he was tempted. "I'll pass," he finally said. "But only because I don't want to upset you all over again.''

Angela held her breath until every last one of them took off, after which she raised her eyes to the heavens and mouthed *Thank you.*

"Return the favor?"

Wincing at Micah's incredulous tone, she mumbled, "I was hoping that would slip by you.''

He stepped closer, his eyes glowing with a strange light. "It didn't.''

She swallowed hard. "Well, I didn't think he'd do it, okay?''

"Pretty sure of yourself, aren't you?"

Feeling his breath stir her hair, Angela stared up at Micah, saw beyond the belligerent expression, got all tangled up in emotions she wanted no part of. She might be sure of herself in most situations, but not with him.

Never with him.

For example, she couldn't be certain which he desired more—to choke her for getting them into a fix...or kiss her for getting them out....

The second thought generated a curious trembling inside her. "We'd better get going...just in case."

Just in case what?

In case Billy Bob changed his mind and came back to take the offered freebie?

In case the state trooper got a line on them and somehow identified her?

Or in case she took a step that would be irreversible...

Angela purposefully stepped back to the car, where she reclaimed her passenger seat, though she was tempted to slide behind the wheel to see what kind of reaction she'd get out of Micah.

Maybe later.

A glance through the rear window told her he was digging around in the trunk, making her regret getting into the car so fast. She'd like to see what he had stored back there. She didn't imagine he'd tell her if she simply asked.

"The printout." Micah handed the sheaf of paper to her and hopped in. "You can play I Spy while I drive." He put the car in Drive. "Sorry I don't own a decoder ring, either."

Scanning the copy on the first page, she sighed. "If you were looking for a way to keep me out of trouble..."

A moment later they merged onto the interstate. Glancing back, Angela got a fleeting impression of a vehicle on the shoulder beneath some trees, but her mind was already preoccupied with the task at hand.

Chapter Nine

"Joey Mariscano has more upstairs than I gave him credit for," Angela admitted much later. "It would take a genius to unravel his personal code in its entirety." More genius than she was capable of at the moment. "Too bad I didn't learn a few secretarial skills in high school. Maybe if I'd taken shorthand..."

"I doubt Mariscano's version would have any relation to the system found in old business textbooks. And I can't imagine you taking notes—or anything else—from anyone."

Having penciled in notes all over the printout of his Las Vegas file, she'd gathered it to be a running transcript of the shady businessman's telephone calls about select operations in her home city. A good night's rest would do wonders for her brain—she could play fill-in-the-blanks and get a more complete narrative. With a sigh, she dumped the sheaf of paper at her feet. She'd worked on the file both before and after their dinner stop. Her eyes were beginning to cross—added to which, night would soon fall.

Enough was enough.

Seven hours plus of concentrated effort and she'd come up with nothing that would further her own defense. Nor did she have a clue as to the identity of Mariscano's chatty Las Vegas contact.

The mysterious Wily?

Discouraged, she stared blankly out over the South Dakota terrain that grew spookier with every mile that passed. The landscape had already taken on a raw quality. Ahead to the west and south, the plains gave way to the barren area known as the Badlands—corrugated stone walls and jagged spires seemingly on fire with the last rays of the setting sun.

"I'm glad there's still some light left," she murmured. Just thinking about traveling through the area after dark was enough to put her on edge.

"Look." Micah indicated a roadside billboard that loomed at them through the growing dusk. "Only twenty-five more miles to Wall Drugs."

He'd pointed out one of the first of the myriad giant announcements back in Minnesota when there'd been five hundred miles to the small town of Wall, their destination for the night. At first she'd made fun of the billboards. Now she thought of them as beacons that reached across the sea of yellow coneflower-dotted prairie. Wall had become an oasis on the other side of the horizon.

Anything that heralded civilization was okay with Angela.

The number of vehicles on the road had decreased and their speed had increased incrementally for every hour since they'd crossed the South Dakota border. The state boasted only two citizens for every square mile, so traffic remained light even around exits to towns. She'd glanced over at the Thunderbird's control panel a while ago—though the digital readout had been seventy-five, other vehicles had been passing them handily.

"I was hoping you were getting somewhere when you found your initials," Micah said, reminding Angela of the promising entry she'd spotted less than an hour ago.

"I did get somewhere, but I'd have to be a mind reader to figure it all out." She shook her head in frustration. As she'd told him earlier, Mariscano indicated he was going to make her a buy-in offer...and then nothing. "Why wouldn't he have kept track of his plans for me?"

"Maybe he started a new file—one I missed."

"Maybe." But it didn't seem likely.

"Tomorrow's another day."

"Right."

Another day closer to her being incarcerated. To learning firsthand what her father's life had been like for nearly twenty years.

For the first time, she wondered how Tomas Dragonetti had felt when he'd been cut off from everything he knew and everyone he loved. And she wondered if he'd ever talked about his feelings with anyone.

For the first time, she wished she could talk about her own feelings with someone.

That someone being Micah Kaminsky, bounty hunter.

Her longing held a certain amount of irony—wanting to be comforted by the very man determined to bring her in.

What was happening to her? How had she grown so soft in only two days?

Opening a vein was not her style. Normally she kept anything questionable—anything that would make her seem weak or vulnerable—to herself. Had Micah been any other man, she had no doubts he would have seen the last of her long ago.

So why hadn't he?

Why was she still with him?

What made her believe he could—and *would*—see her through this mess until the end?

Wanting in the worst way to understand his power over her, she suddenly asked, "Who are you really?" She fleetingly thought of Mesmer, the controversial German physician who had developed the use of "animal magnetism" or hypnosis in psychotherapy.

Micah started. "What do you mean?"

Noting the odd strain in his voice, she said, "You're a confusing man, Kaminsky. I started out being afraid of you."

"And now?"

And now she couldn't imagine why. "You're no pussycat, but you're not a slathering beast, either."

His posture relaxed. He laughed, the timbre of his voice and the slight dimple in his right cheek culling a response from some mysterious place deep inside her. Her heart beat a little faster.

"Slathering beast, huh? I've been called a lot of things, but—"

"Like what?"

She had a sudden need to know everything about Micah, even the ignominious names he'd had thrown at him.

"*Rough around the edges,* for one. And then there's *pod person*—"

"I didn't exactly call you that," she objected.

"But my personal favorite is *bozo.*"

Reminded of the woman trucker, Angela chuckled. "I could go with that, if you like."

"The Dragonlady asks my permission?"

Her smile faded. "Is that how I appear to you?"

"Sometimes."

"Nothing like brutal honesty."

"I can lie if you want."

"I hate lies."

"I sensed that," he said, jaw tightening for a moment. Then he cleared his throat, and though he seemed to be staring straight ahead, she was certain he was casing her. "I prefer Angel myself."

Angela thought of her double-decade bias against the nickname her father had given her. Somehow she didn't mind it so much coming from Micah.

"Angel as in...heavenly?" she joked. "I find it hard to believe you see anything positive in me." After all, she certainly hadn't given him reason.

"Call it insight. Under other circumstances..."

Under other circumstances, Angela knew she wouldn't have given Micah Kaminsky the time of day. She would have been too busy polishing the armor protecting her soft side to notice more than his good looks. And what a waste that would have been. She would have missed his quick wit...his humor...his affinity with gadgetry and his strange attachment to a vehicle far past its prime.

When Angela vaguely wondered what she might have missed about Douglas and whether or not she would care if she knew, tentacles of guilt wrapped around her. Here she was, wanting to get closer to another man while the one she had was too far away to do anything but worry himself sick over her.

What kind of a person was she?

Micah's hearty "Welcome to Wall" drove the question from her mind. They'd just entered the town limits.

"Civilization," she breathed with a sigh of relief. "At long last."

"I had the feeling you were less than thrilled with our

surroundings the last couple of hundred miles. You'd think you'd never been on a wide-open road before, when Nevada is full of them.''

Roads she neatly avoided. "When I leave Las Vegas, it's to fly to San Francisco or Dallas or New York." She glanced at him when she added, "Or Chicago.''

Oddly disappointed at his lack of reaction, she shifted around in the seat that was starting to feel as if it was made of lumps. Maybe Micah wasn't from Chicago. She knew so little about him.

"When you were a kid, didn't you ever go camping?''

"You mean outside where things could creep and crawl over me when I'm asleep?" She shuddered. "Please.''

"Hmm. Thinking about camping makes me visualize the stars overhead and wonderful night sounds carrying on the breeze.''

"Like coyotes howling?''

"Exactly.''

"Oh, that's different, then." She rolled her eyes, then froze. "Hey, you're not getting any weird ideas about saving a few bucks, are you?''

He choked back a laugh. "Don't worry, we're sleeping indoors tonight.''

After securing a room at another no-name motel at the edge of town—at least it was a clean one this time— Micah suggested they stretch their legs at the now infamous Wall Drugs, which he described as a potpourri of connected stores selling mostly Western memorabilia.

Either he'd seen the place before or he'd been reading travel brochures in some men's room along the way.

Even though darkness was descending rapidly, Angela could tell his face was looking drawn again. Unless his not shaving made him look so tired. His five-o'clock shadow had progressed to some serious growth. Still, she was concerned, especially since he wouldn't consider letting her drive.

"What about sleep?"

"I was thinking we'd find clothes for you first. But we need to hurry. The town'll probably shut down in another hour or so."

Angela set on the dresser the cans of soda they'd gotten out of a machine. Asking "In a tourist place, how far can twenty bucks go?" she crossed to the window where the drapes were only half-closed.

"Maybe I can loosen the purse strings a little."

Thinking about the luxury of material that was clean and soft against her skin infused her spirits with anticipation. Before snapping the drapes together, she barely noted a vehicle pulling up in front of the motel office.

"Give me time to shower first. I promise I'll be quick."

"Go. I'll catch up with the news." He switched on the television anchored to the wall.

Angela was nearly euphoric. Clean body. Clean clothes. She grabbed a can of soda to take into the bathroom with her. What more could she ask for?

Uh-oh.

Of course there had to be a hitch.

"Ahem. I need a hand. Two, actually. This gown isn't exactly a do-it-yourself deal."

"My pleasure."

Micah's agreeable response swept through her like a heated caress. And he was gazing at her through slitted eyes, his expression sexy and suggestive.

Wishing he'd left the mirrored sunglasses on so she couldn't tell what he was thinking, she spun around on her heel, presenting him with her back. That way he wouldn't notice the rising color that had to be creeping up her neck to her ears. She pressed the can of soda to her throat, hoping to cool herself down. But as he undid the tiny buttons at the top of the bodice, his fingers brushed her skin.

Her sensitive flesh responded instantly.

She covered her quick intake of breath by clearing her throat and shifting.

"Something wrong?" he asked,

"Dust," she lied. "I'm allergic to it."

"And you live in the southwest?"

"It's a different kind of dust than you have around here."

"Sure it is. Sand is infinitely less irritating." He unzipped the material. "Good grief, you're being held captive by a Merry Widow."

"Believe me, there's nothing merry about being stuck in this thing for days at a time."

"I can only imagine." He started unhooking it. "So why have you?"

Aware of each of his fingers on her even as a surfeit of air began to fill her lungs, she said, "I haven't exactly had any options."

"In the early seventies, women burned their bras."

A liberating thought.

She swallowed hard. "Got a match?"

Catching the front of the gown and corset to her, she held her breath and clenched her jaw against the sensations rocking her as Micah undid the last of the hooks. His fingers lingered in the hollow at the small of her back a tad too long for her comfort. Warmth bloomed and spread through her middle and threatened the rest of her if she didn't do something to break the contact *now*.

She practically jumped away from him.

"Thanks." Physically exposed and emotionally vulnerable, she wasted no time. She scooted into the bathroom with the promise "I'll only be a few minutes" tumbling from her lips.

Inside, she flipped the door closed and leaned against it to catch the breath that she'd somehow lost again. Of course she'd be quick.

After all, how long could anyone stand a cold shower?

THINKING BETTER of leaving the room at all, Micah tried using the televised news to busy his mind and to bring his body some relief from the instant frustration he'd experienced on touching Angela. He sat in a rickety armchair before the television, but failed to concentrate.

Instead, he thought about buying her new clothes. He should have found a way earlier. Helping her out of the gown had been a test of his inner strength. He had a special affinity for lingerie, and the corset had nearly undone him. He didn't know how he'd restrained himself from taking her in his arms and making love to her...if she would have let him.

He suspected his odds were pretty good.

And then what?

Angela Dragon wasn't the kind of woman a man made love to, then walked out on. And what other choice would he have? When she knew who he was—understood *what* he was—she'd want nothing more to do with him. He couldn't tolerate the thought of her looking at him with the same cold, angry expression she wore when talking about her father.

He wiped a hand over his face as the truth hit him.

How could he have let this happen? If he thought traveling with her had been rough before...

The screech of the plumbing made him start. Not wanting to listen to Angela's shower noises, to imagine her soaping her naked body—something he'd dearly love to do himself—Micah increased the volume on the television, reminding himself they weren't supposed to have been attracted to each other, and he wasn't supposed to have become personally involved.

He'd merely been returning a favor...squaring accounts...performing what he'd thought of as a piece-of-cake assignment.

There weren't supposed to be all these damnable variables.

Micah sighed. He guessed fate wasn't particularly responsive to man's demands. He, of all people, should know that by now. No matter how he'd tried to live his life, from the start fate had had other ideas for him.

He forced himself to watch the news.

Another skirmish in the Middle East...

A national campaign against teenage smoking...

A local politician caught with his pants down...

He didn't really give the tube his full attention until he was jerked from his passivity by Angela glaring at him from the television screen.

Or rather, glaring at the reporters barraging her for a story.

"The trial of Angela Dragon may be put on hold," the anchorwoman was saying as a knock came at the motel-room door. "After being indicted on Thursday afternoon, Dragon dropped out of sight."

The shot pulled out to show her surrounded by family, her lawyer and a fair-haired man with a possessive posture. Micah sat up straighter. He'd forgotten that Angela had claimed she'd used his cell phone to call her supposed fiancé.

"According to our sources, she jumped bail and may be fleeing across country with this man."

An old mug shot filled the screen.

And Micah's fingers dug deep into the arms of his chair.

The rest of the story was lost to him. He couldn't focus on the voice. Couldn't make sense of the words. He was aware of a pounding sound coming from somewhere, but he put it down to his own phobic heartbeat.

He was being implicated in another crime...but how? Who was this source? Only one person had been privy to his plans. The man who'd sent him on this mission.

The walls began closing in on him until the room felt as airless as a jail cell.

The noise was magnified until he realized it was coming from outside himself. From outside the motel room. A crash followed by a splintering of wood got his complete attention. Micah whipped out of the chair.

The door had caved in with little trouble.

And two men were coming for him.

CLEANLINESS WAS definitely a virtue, Angela decided as she wrapped a towel around her hair and dried herself off.

Raised voices in the other room caught her attention, but she attributed them to the television.

Her clothes littered the small floor where she'd stepped out of them. And the only things she was willing to step back into were her dress and shoes—and for propriety's sake, her high-cut briefs. She put them on first, shoes next. No more corset! She stuffed the thing into the wastebasket along with her ripped pantyhose. Micah was resourceful. He'd get her back into the gown somehow.

A heavy weight whomping against the bathroom door and nearly popping it from its hinges was her first clue the din in the other room wasn't coming from the television, after all.

"Micah?"

Suddenly alarmed, she nearly flung the door open until she realized she was next to naked. She struggled into the dress, fighting to get her arms through the holes.

A crash and loud grunt knotted her stomach and stole her breath. A thief must have broken in to their room.

Instinctively, she looked around for a weapon, but neither the tiny soap bars nor the plastic wastebasket seemed as if they'd be the least effective. Her panicked gaze lit on the full can of soda. Hanging on to the front of the gown with one hand and grabbing the weighty soft drink can with the other, she cracked open the door as a dark-clad body went flying past in a blur.

Adrenaline pumping, she flung the panel wide to see a second man in dark clothing with his hands around Micah's throat. Like a lioness protecting her young, she let go a screech that came from deep inside. The villain started, head turning toward her as she pulled back her arm.

She stared him straight in his beady eyes as she flung the can of soda.

He ducked.

Micah didn't—the can bounced off his temple, whipping his head back.

"Oh, my god!" Distressed at the unfortunate hit, she picked up the dresser lamp and charged the villain.

At the same time, Micah recouped and grabbed the man's shirt. Whipping him around, he smashed his fist into the attacker's nose. Blood spurted everywhere.

And the villain sprawled back against the nightstand,

knocked over the telephone, which flew against the wall, and crumpled to the floor unconscious.

Angela would have gone after his partner, but the second man had already beaten a retreat through the open door. And from the sound of the squeal of tires, she suspected he didn't have much loyalty for his cohort.

"What's going on?" came a faint woman's voice from somewhere nearby.

"I don't know," a disgruntled-sounding man answered, "but I'm gonna find out. I need my sleep tonight!"

Setting down the lamp, she took a strangled breath as she caught sight of Micah's face, streaked with blood, his temple already discoloring. She'd done that to him.

Fisting the gown's bodice to her chest, she asked, "Are you all right?"

"No thanks to you," Micah said wryly, already searching the man he'd downed.

She winced. "I was aiming for *him*."

He removed both a knife and a gun. "That's a comfort." Then he went through the man's pockets.

Even as he checked over the objects he removed, she started for the telephone. "I'll ask the night manager to get the local authorities over here."

"No!" he said sharply.

Angela stared at him, a growing fear holding her to the spot. Instinctively she knew the men weren't thieves preying on tourists.

"What's going on, Micah?"

Staring at a wrinkled scrap of paper, he muttered, "They've caught up to us."

"They, who?"

Rather than answering, he rose and moved toward the bathroom where light poured out the door. He showed her the piece of notepaper decorated with the Joshua tree and coyote—familiar symbols in Nevada—across which was scrawled WX 9428.

"My license plate number."

He shoved the paper into his pocket.

So the men had been on their trail. For how long? Since Chicago?

"Is it really *us* they're interested in?" she asked. "Or just me?"

"I'd say it's a toss-up."

Which meant they both could have been killed....

And suddenly Angela didn't feel like playing heroine anymore, not when the rules weren't negotiable. If being shot at once hadn't put the fear of God into her, she was feeling all too mortal now. Looking at Micah made her feel even worse. And determined.

"We need to bring the authorities in on this."

"No."

"This is more than we can handle, Micah. It's more than *I* can handle."

She stared into the face that had become so familiar to her and hardly recognized it for all the bruising and blood. Taking a chance with her own life was one thing. Taking a chance with someone else's—his—was another.

"If we call in the authorities and tell them what's going on," she said, pushing past the lump forming in her throat, "they'll put guards on me until they get me back to Nevada."

"If they believe you."

"Why wouldn't they?"

"Why wouldn't they believe someone set you up in the first place?"

She shrugged. "They didn't have proof."

"They still don't."

"The real criminal is on to me." Her succeeding at whatever she'd put her hand to in the past had convinced her she could do anything, but now she had to reevaluate. To be honest with herself. "The way my luck has gone so far, I don't see how I'm going to figure out *who* that person is, no less get anything on him to clear my name."

"I'll help you."

The unexpected offer gave her a start. Meeting Micah's intense gaze, she wondered about his change of heart. Before, he'd been willing to leave her fate to the justice system. She supposed she'd grown on him, as he had on her. A taste of shared danger had had some kind of bonding effect on them both. That had to be it—the reason for their newly formed trust in each other.

Or was it something far more personal?

Blood suddenly rushed to her head, confusing her. And before she could respond to Micah's offer, raised voices outside caught Angela's attention.

"I'm telling you, it sounded like a house coming down," the disgruntled man was saying.

"The deputy is on his way now," returned a younger man, whom she took to be the night manager.

"C'mon, Angel, let's go while the going is good."

Hoping she wasn't making a mistake in letting Micah talk her out of turning herself in, Angela was nevertheless tempted to rip the name of the man who'd hired him from the attacker's throat. A quick look to the floor near the nightstand told her he wasn't where he'd fallen. She whipped around in a circle, searching the room's shadows.

"He's gone," she said incredulously. "He got out of

here without us knowing." They'd been too intent on each other to pay him any mind.

Micah was already at the door. "Hurry!"

Still hanging on to the front of her gown so the bodice would stay in place, she rushed from the room, trying not to look in the direction of the two men just outside the door.

"Hey, you!" yelled the disgruntled one.

The motel manager cleared his throat. "Excuse me, sir…"

But Micah waited for no one. The car was humming even as he slid behind the wheel and Angela flew into the passenger seat. As they drove off, her mind raced as fast as her pulse. She looked around for either attacker, but both seemed to have disappeared into thin air.

As they escaped the grounds, the disgruntled man dispatched a rude hand gesture in their direction, while the manager ran into their room, undoubtedly to check on the damage.

Their whizzing by the motel office jump-started Angela's memory. "A tan Jeep…"

"What about it?"

"When I was closing the drapes, I saw one in front of the office."

Micah glanced through the rear window as though he could spot the vehicle. "The same bastards who tried to run you down at the strip mall this morning?"

"Exactly."

Jaw clenched, he sped away as if he could leave impending trouble behind, making a couple of fast turns that got them on a dark road.

Everything began clicking into place for Angela. She realized they'd been made back in Minnesota—the two men watching them from beneath the tree at the state

park had known who they were. Is that where they'd
picked up Micah's license number? But how had they
known where to pick up her trail?

Who had known...?

And why was Micah so reluctant to call in the authorities, considering the bad guys seemed to be playing
for keeps? She had the weirdest feeling he wasn't telling
her everything, but Angela knew that, for once in her
life, she had to trust someone other than herself.

Chapter Ten

When Wall was nothing more than a shimmer of light behind them, Angela asked, "Where are we headed?"

"Where the bastards won't find us."

Which looked to be straight for the vast Badlands.

A chill shot through her as she faced moonlight-silvered behemoths of fossil-rich mudstone. Rising before them were jagged spires, buttes and towers, a vista so foreign they might be heading for another planet.

And they weren't on a paved road.

"You've been here before?"

"Not exactly."

"Then how do you know where you're going?"

Her words vibrated with each rut they crossed. She clenched her jaw to keep her teeth from clacking together.

"Instinct."

In other words, Angela decided, stomach churning, Micah didn't have a clue.

But he kept on as if he did, eventually finding another asphalt-covered road. Heavy silence stretched between them as they further invaded the lunar landscape. Mile after mile they traveled deeper into foreign territory, eerie and glowing silver-blue.

Angela almost felt as if she were outside of herself—outside of the experience—as if she were watching a movie. Or having a dream.

A bad dream.

The culmination of a living nightmare.

When Micah finally slowed, she thought he would admit he was lost, but he was purposely pulling off the paved road onto a dirt track that cut through a flat area with some growth. When they came to a wide clearing, he stopped the car and cut the engine. Before he turned them off, the headlights picked up the gleam of water at the bottom of a modest incline.

Following his lead, she left the car and started toward the creek. "You wouldn't have a map of this area?"

"Not detailed. And not that it matters. I'm not planning on going anywhere until daybreak."

"You're kidding, right?"

Suddenly her heel caught on the cracked earth and she teetered between falling and losing her modesty. Seeing her predicament, Micah caught her, his hands warm and steady on her arms. Now she was in danger of losing her focus. Of forgetting where she was. Who she was. She wanted in the worst way to be held. Sheltered.

To forget she was a Dragonlady.

To forget she was a fugitive from the law…

"Turn around and let me fix that," he coaxed. "Why didn't you tell me you needed a hand?"

"During which convenient part of the evening?" But turn she did, her heart beating faster as his fingertips found the hollow at her waist. "You don't really plan on spending the night out here, do you?"

"It's as good a place as any," he said, starting to zip the gown. "Suck in."

Though she pulled in her breath, she managed to protest, "A room with a bed would be as good a place as any."

He faltered, the zipper halfway up. "We don't have one of those."

"We could find one." Too aware of his hand in the middle of her back, his breath stirring her hair, she whispered, "Uh, the zipper..."

"I don't think we'll find too many on Indian land."

Trying to break the tension with humor, she asked, "Zippers? Uh, what do you mean by *Indian land?*"

"Motels, not zippers." Micah completed the task. "And if we're not on the Pine Ridge Reservation yet, we're headed in that direction." He turned her around and brushed his fingers over what was left of the sleeves. "I think."

"Oh."

They stared at each other until Angela wondered if he wasn't going to do something about the high-wire tension building between them. Moonlight and shadow played over his battered features. He appeared intense. Hungry, though not for food. Ready to take what she was willing to give.

Angela could hardly believe herself. Could hardly believe what she was considering. She wanted to give more to a man she'd known for only two days than she had to the one she'd been seeing for months.

The reminder of Douglas broke the connection. Once she lowered her eyes, Micah turned away. Hunkering down, he sliced both hands into the creek and wet his face. She could hardly miss his sharp intake of breath.

"Micah?" Concerned, she sank down next to him, reached out and cupped his chin. "My, you do look wretched."

"Thanks to you," he reminded her.

"Let me help you now."

Ripping a hunk of material from the front of her skirt, she dunked the cloth in the icy stream.

"I don't want to hear how this is going to hurt you more than it does me."

"Okay, then…how about 'Whatever doesn't kill you will make you stronger'?" she joked.

From the way his muscles tensed when she gently blotted his face, she figured no one would ever compare her to Florence Nightingale. Her "Sorry" encompassed not only the hurt she was causing him now, but the fact that she'd put him in jeopardy in the first place.

She started to pull her hand away.

He caught her wrist.

Again they stared at each other. A faint animal cry in the distance raised the hair on her arms.

Or was it his touch?

"I thought you always finished what you started," he said, freeing her.

Too aware of his close inspection, Angela lifted the lock of damp hair away from his forehead and, folding the cloth and dunking it back into the water, placed the makeshift cold pack over the discolored area.

"Not too bad," she said. "A few bruises. A split lip. Most of the blood came from the bastard's nose. I think you'll live."

"Thanks for the positive prognosis. Haven't you ever heard the adage 'Kiss it and make it better'?"

Warmth flooded her. And an awkwardness Angela wasn't used to. Her pulse threaded wildly.

How could she resist the suggestion…or the challenge in his eyes?

Removing the cloth, she brushed her lips across his temple, worked her way down below his eye and cheek, and nuzzled his split lip. Though it was already healing, the cut tasted salty. His breath spilled across her mouth. Certain that he meant to kiss her, Angela sighed and closed her eyes....

And could hardly believe it when Micah wrenched himself away from her.

Eyes flashing open, she stared up at him. Seeming to have removed himself mentally from their brief connection, he was holding out his hand to her. Dazed, she placed her fingers along his palm and allowed him to grab her and help her up. Once she was on her feet, however, he immediately let go and turned away.

"I have some things in the car to make the ground more comfortable. We'd better get some sleep if we're going to be on our way by dawn."

The bounty hunter certainly knew how to kill a mood, Angela decided. Added to which, he had made her feel utterly foolish. Their situation was anything but romantic, true. The setting was downright gothic. Miffed anyway, she flounced after him, determined to get a peek into the Thunderbird's mysterious cavity. But even as she caught up to Micah, whose arms were already full, he slammed the trunk shut.

Clenching her jaw, Angela determined to get a good night's rest despite him.

AN IDLE THREAT.

Between the coyotes howling and the wind soughing through the canyon, the closest Angela got to sleep was a hazy in-between state. Though Micah had given her the only foam pad and one of two blankets, they hadn't been enough to make her feel comfortable and secure. Certain that somewhere in the wild a snake had her name, she hadn't been able to rid herself of the notion that it might sneak a night's warmth by crawling under the covers with her.

Her mind drifted off and on but refused to let go completely. Therefore, when Micah rose from his bedding that he'd set a few yards from hers, she was immediately aware of his movements.

Not wanting him to know she wasn't asleep, she kept her breath even and watched him through nearly closed lashes. He dived into the backpack he'd been using as a makeshift pillow and produced his cell phone, then moved away from their small camp area. He perched on a rock, his back to her.

Who in the world could he be calling in the middle of the night?

Wondering if he had a wife or girlfriend—a possibility she hadn't considered before—Angela strained to hear his end of the conversation. At first she found it impossible to tune in. But gradually she was able to focus, to catch a few words here and there.

"Only now I'm not so sure."

What wasn't he sure about? she wondered. His relationship with this other woman?

"I was afraid of that...."

Afraid of what? She listened harder.

"...have to know what's up..."

She continued to assume he was speaking to some possible love interest—undoubtedly the reason he'd rejected her—until she heard him say, "Called in a favor..."

And then there was something about Chicago. Unease crept through her.

"No one the wiser..." he was saying. The word *trouble* came loud and clear. And a few seconds later "...what he really wanted."

Who? What who wanted?

"Angela doesn't know what's going on...."

Hearing her name was like a siren going off. Her pulse shot up like a geyser. All her senses went on alert. Wanting in the worst way to get up and demand an immediate explanation, she forced herself to lie there as if she were dead to the world.

She caught "Hot Springs" and "eastern Wyoming" before he rose and turned her way. He mumbled something else, then apparently ended the conversation, because he lowered the cell phone. Though she shut her eyes completely, she felt his powerful gaze on her, piercing the dark as if he could see she was awake.

Angela took a deep, audible breath and rolled over to her side as she might do if she really were sleeping. Eyes still closed, she sensed rather than saw Micah standing over her. Her heart pounded so loudly she was certain he heard. A light sweat covered her despite the night's chill.

Only hours ago she'd been open to giving herself to Micah, and now he made her afraid. But of what exactly, she wasn't certain. Angela decided it wasn't the man himself she feared, so much as what he might be up to.

She knew the exact moment he moved away back toward his bedding, and she chanced a peek through slitted lashes. He hovered over the backpack for a moment and pulled out something—a towel?—then moved off in the direction of the creek.

Odd that he had the urge to bathe when he should be trying to get some sleep.

It was all Angela could do to keep herself from jumping up and following him, pummeling him for some answers, but she restrained herself in order to get her hands on the cell phone. She knew exactly how to find out who he'd called. Waiting only until she heard the first splash of water, she threw off the cover and sneaked over to his blanket. He'd dropped the phone on top of the backpack. Her eyes already having adjusted to the bright moonlight, she switched it on and quickly hit the Redial function.

Her pulse raced as she waited for a connection. Two rings and the receiver on the other end lifted. Not knowing what to expect, she held her breath...

"Hello?"

And nearly choked at the familiar voice.

"Hello, is someone there?"

Angela opened her mouth to answer, but for once in her life, words failed her.

Hand shaking, she hung up without even thinking.

Then her mind began racing.

What in the world had Micah been doing talking to her mother?

She fought the first thought that came to mind. No matter that she tried to forget the ridiculous notion, she couldn't ease it away. What if Micah had called her mother demanding money for her safe return? That way he could go through with their agreement and not turn her in, while receiving the reward he'd set out to get in the first place.

But she had offered to pay him to let her go, Angela thought, puzzled.

Though he'd turned down the offer of money, he *had* shown interest in a more personal reward....

This was ridiculous. She was guessing. That it had been her mother whom Micah had called both relieved and scared her. She ought to ask him directly what he was about. Only, she knew she wouldn't. She didn't trust him to tell her the truth.

Trust.

Always a shaky issue with her.

Turning the cell phone back on, she punched in the number of someone who'd never given her reason to doubt him. When Douglas didn't answer, she tried his cellular number.

A moment later a sleep-filled voice murmured, "Yeah?"

Relieved that he'd kept his cell phone nearby, she said, "Sorry I woke you."

"Angela!" Immediately sounding wide awake, he demanded, "Are you all right? Are you back in Las Vegas?"

"Yes to the first, no to the second. I'm fine, despite the fact that I'm holed up in the middle of the Badlands, probably on some Indian reservation." Knowing how sounds carried in the open, she was careful to keep her voice low. "Not that *where* matters."

"Of course it matters," Douglas said indignantly. "What's Kaminsky thinking?"

If only she knew.

Reminded of Micah's proximity, she pricked up her ears. Continued splashing sounds assured her he was still busy at the creek, but who knew for how long. She needed to get down to business.

"Douglas, have you heard anything about Frank Gonnella?"

"I had the P.I. check him out like you asked. He called earlier. Word on the street is Gonnella's homesick for the old days. I guess running a car dealership doesn't satisfy his craving for excitement."

"Then he's worked himself out of retirement?"

"We don't have anything concrete yet. One day's not

a lot of time. And at the moment Gonnella himself is out of town visiting his daughter in Wyoming."

"Wyoming…so close," she murmured.

Close enough to supervise the operation to shut her mouth, Angela decided, then remembered Micah saying something about eastern Wyoming to her mother.

Did he know something she didn't?

"There's also a rumor that not so long ago Gonnella held a financial interest in Picture Perfect," Douglas was saying.

The photography-video company that had gotten her into all this trouble!

"Oh, my God, if that's true…"

Angela hoped it meant she could present the prosecution with a convincing case in her own defense.

"I hope to get a confirmation by tomorrow."

"Douglas, you're a wonder."

"Right," he said wryly. "The same wonder who got you into the deal."

"Stop blaming yourself."

"How can I? Maybe if I could hold you in my arms…"

Guilt shot through Angela. If only she had the same longing. Fool that she was, even now she longed for a different pair of arms.

A far more muscular, sensual set of arms.

Still, she said, "It'll only be another couple of days."

And nights. Caught by the whole heaven of stars overhead, the likes of which she'd never seen before, she stifled thoughts of spending those nights in Micah's company.

"What the hell's wrong with that recovery agent?" Douglas yelled, not bothering to soft-soap his anger. "Why hasn't he flown you back here?"

"I get the feeling he doesn't fly in anything but his Thunderbird." She perked up her ears. No more splashing sounds. Thinking she'd better cut the conversation short, she asked, "Douglas, what about the other man I told you about? The guy named Wily?"

"Hard to get a bead on that one, not even a last name. Your Wily's a real mystery man. A mercenary who hires himself out to the highest bidder. And he seems to have disappeared off the streets of Las Vegas."

"Then he could be anywhere."

In a train station...or behind the wheel of a tan Jeep.

"Angela, please let me talk to the authorities in your behalf. It's time you stopped playing fast and loose with your life, don't you think?"

"You're right. I know you are."

"But...?"

Footsteps crunching along the dry earth told her Micah was on his way back to camp.

"But I've got to go," she whispered, not wanting Micah to nail her again. "I'll find a way to call you tomorrow, probably from somewhere in Wyoming."

She clicked off in the midst of Douglas's frustrated objections. Dropping the cell phone where she'd found it, she eased herself back to her own bedding and continued her pretense of being asleep.

As much as she'd like to face Micah down about the call to her mother, now was neither the time nor the place to push the issue. She was too upset, too confused. Not at all in control the way she wanted to be.

She *would* find her moment.

Meanwhile, Douglas had renewed her hope...and had given her restless brain plenty to mull over while she lay awake all night.

"ANGEL, WAKE UP."

Wrapped in a cottony haze, having barely fallen asleep, she muttered, "Go away."

"Exactly what I plan to do as soon as you get up. Do it slow. No sudden moves."

Her eyes flashed open. "What?"

"Easy. Real easy."

Fearing their attackers had caught up to them, she forced her brain awake and did as he said, slowly sitting up. The breath caught in her throat. Danger stood all around them in the forms of dozens of huge, ugly beasts. A whole herd of them, many whose mangy, oversize heads hung to the ground while they foraged on edible grasses.

"Buffalo?"

"Bison. They came for water from the creek. They're not particularly friendly animals...and they're easily excitable."

Great. She'd survived a would-be assassin, a near hit-and-run and motel muggers—not to mention the snake with her name—only to face a potential stampede. Shoes in hand, she slipped to her feet and cautiously took a few steps back on the hard-caked earth.

"What about the bedding?" she whispered.

One of the unkempt beasts was already snorting all over hers.

"The blanket's expendable. You're not."

"I'm touched."

She inched toward the car, as instructed making no sudden moves. One of the bison turned baleful eyes on her, snorted and pawed the ground. Her heart thundered in her breast.

"Angel-l-l." Micah was already at the car.

"I'm doing the best I can," she protested, inching faster.

Only when she neared the Thunderbird did she notice the backpack on the ground where Micah had left it. She pulled a face. No doubt the cellular phone was still inside—it, too, being superfluous.

How was she supposed to get in touch with Douglas, as she'd promised?

Calling collect in the middle of the wilderness would be quite a trick.

A loud snort and baleful cry put wings to her feet. Heart in her throat, she flew into the car even as the irate bison rushed it. He turned to the side at the last second, though his powerful shoulder grazed the fender. The vehicle bounced on its shocks.

"Can we get out of here?" she begged. "Now?"

"Your wish..."

As if she could command him to do anything.

Angela didn't settle down inside until the herd was safely behind them.

"So you think this camping thing will catch on?"

"You have no appreciation for nature, Angel. Think about the awesomeness of waking up in the middle of a bison herd. How many people can say they've done that?"

"I don't know. How many lived to tell?"

The sun was rising over the horizon, casting deep and defining shadows throughout the peaks and canyons of the Badlands. A panorama of color played across the seemingly barren mudstone. Shafts of light painted the layers of sediment with purple, red and gold—the brilliant colors presenting a startling contrast to the deep green of the closer grasslands, prickly prairie that the bison had left temporarily to quench their thirst.

Angela ignored her own thirst and hunger and gave in to the heavy-lidded feeling that came of not having had enough sleep.

She drifted in and out for a while, finally awakening to find they'd left the north wall behind. The vista had changed yet again, flattened land around them thick with tall grasses. Ahead, pale brown bodies leaped through a field of pink coneflowers.

"Pronghorns," Micah said. "And over there..." He pointed off to her right. "A golden eagle."

Wings spread wide, the magnificent bird soared on an updraft. She watched for a moment, mesmerized.

But even in the face of such an awesome sight, she couldn't smother her empty-stomach testiness. "Are we there yet?"

"Define there."

"Any place with food."

"Coming up."

She sank back into silence, finding a grudging appreciation in the raw beauty of her surroundings. And amidst nature's splendor, bits of fenced and farmed land encircled scattered houses that reflected their owners' poverty. A quarter of an hour later they entered a small town whose Native American roots were made obvious by the bronze-skinned citizens going about their business.

No doubt about their being on reservation land.

They stopped at a combination gas station, grocery store and fast-food joint. Angela's tour of the ladies' room convinced her she was a hopeless case. What was left of her gown was tattered and dusty, her skin was dirt streaked and her hair poked out wildly. She washed up anyway and ran damp hands through her hair, making certain to camouflage the bald spot.

Getting food was a self-service operation. Micah handed her money and told her to knock herself out. While she waited for coffee, eggs and fry bread, he got on the pay telephone near the rest rooms.

Who could he be calling now? Surely not her mother again.

But it seemed he wasn't successful in getting through to his party. His expression reflecting his frustration, he slammed the receiver into its cradle just as she arrived at the cashier's station.

The Lakota woman sitting behind the cash register inspected her thoroughly and made no attempt to hide her amusement as she took the twenty and made change. Her wide grin filled her broad-cheeked face.

"Some honeymoon, huh?"

"It's been a real hoot."

Angela didn't miss the speculative gleam in the other woman's eyes as Micah arrived in time to carry the food tray. He looked big and wild—thanks to the two days of beard growth—and irresistibly sexy. She followed directly behind him, muttering to herself about having more hormones than brains.

Micah set the tray on an empty table and gave her a quizzical look. "Did you say something?"

Not about to repeat the self-observation, she said, "I was wondering who you called."

"Would you believe the motor club?"

"No." Not that she would recognize the truth should he ever tell it. "Try again."

"The weather?"

Ticked at his continuing evasiveness, she asked, "They make predictions for the middle of nowhere?"

"Movie times."

Her voice rose sharply as she asked, "Is that the best you can do?"

Heat rose along her neck when Micah started. Angela acknowledged she was acting weird. Even before she had got to know him personally, when she would have done anything to get away from him, she hadn't felt so...irritable.

So...disappointed.

Trying to work up some righteous anger of the sort she was used to was an exercise in frustration. Something had changed between them and she suspected they could never go back to the way things had been.

Correction. *She* could never go back.

Angela wasn't certain what *he* was capable of.

Quietly, expression serious, he asked, "What is it you want, Angel?"

"How about the truth?"

But he couldn't seem to manage it.

"Are you always this cranky when you're hungry?" He gestured to the food. "Sit and eat."

She should have known better than to give him a crumb of honesty. Glaring, she took a seat and wolfed down her eggs and fry bread with a vengeance, then waited for him to catch up. All the while, he seemed as if he had something to say to her, yet he remained equally silent.

More silence strained the hour's drive to Hot Springs. Angela was surprised when he slowed down and tooled around town like a tourist. They passed turn-of-the-century homes, resort hotels and sanatoriums, many of the older structures built of sandstone.

"What are we doing here?" she asked, even as she admired the buildings' intricate carvings and ornamental designs.

"Looking for the ATM."

"*The* ATM?"

"They're few and far between in this part of the country. We probably won't have another chance to get money until we hit Cheyenne or Denver."

He found the cash station outside a bank. Figuring she had a day of straight driving ahead of her, Angela left the car also to stretch her legs and back.

Vaguely aware of a dark sedan pulling in to the lot, she paid it no mind as she paced back and forth, trying to get rid of the stiffness already binding her muscles. But when a second similar car rolled in, she took better notice, since most vehicles in these parts were built to withstand unpaved roads.

These were city cars.

Internal radar blipping, she turned to alert Micah as two men walked up to the cash machine, the scrawny one looking around, the bigger one intent on him. The stranger's hands were gloved and the right one wasn't empty.

"Hey, you!" she yelled.

Too late. His arm swung, the weapon in his hand cracking Micah across the back of the head. He went down like a sack of potatoes.

Angela choked on his name and tried to run to him. A hand grasped her arm and brought her to an abrupt halt.

She swung around to face a mean-looking bear of a man, one narrowed eye distorted by a nasty scar. Her pulse leaped as she recognized him.

"Mr. Mariscano wants you should come with me to see him."

Not that Adolpho gave her any choice.

Chapter Eleven

Joey Mariscano was pacing the length of the hunting lodge's great hall like a caged animal when he heard the cars pull up.

Caged. The very word made him shudder.

Business notwithstanding, he was a careful man. He indulged in neither unnecessary violence nor slipshod operations. Sometimes one goal conflicted with the other.

That happening made Joey decidedly unhappy.

He took a big breath and seated himself in the largest of the chairs bookending the couch and the stone fireplace. The furniture was primitive—lots of chunky wood and Indian-blanket upholstery. His own taste ran to fine leather and highly polished surfaces, but this wasn't his call.

The door banged open and a decidedly unkempt Angela Dragon flew inside, propelled by Adolpho's hamlike hand. Filling the doorway, his lieutenant looked as if he might enjoy hurting the woman to get her to talk.

"That's enough," Joey said, staring at what was left of the wedding gown.

"Sure, boss."

"You find it?"

"Nah, not yet, but the boys'll take the T-bird apart."

"Good."

"What about the other one? He's out for now, but you want I should take care of it so he stays that way permanently?"

Joey sighed. Adolpho was from the old school and stubbornly clung to his narrow views of organized crime. "Just have him brought in."

Adolpho backed out of the room.

The Dragon woman was trying not to shake. "Micah's alive, then?"

He could see that meant a lot to her. And after Kaminsky had dragged her out of the expo center like some kind of caveman. Surprise, surprise.

"So far he is."

No sense in letting her think he was soft, because he wasn't. He was smart, was all. Smart enough to cover his tracks and keep his butt out of the slammer.

"What are you going to do to us?"

"Now, that's up to you." He gazed at her intently when he said, "You took something that belongs to me."

Her pained expression when she asked, "As in...?" was blatantly put on.

"A little black book."

"Girlfriends?" She managed to sound shocked. "Does DeeDee know about this?"

The reminder of the way she'd set off his daughter didn't please him. "You got a mouth on you. Close it unless you're ready to deal."

"Sorry." She tried sounding contrite. Standing in back of the other chair, she fingered the material, the only evidence of her nerves. "What makes you think I have this black book of yours?"

He put a beringed hand into his breast suit pocket and pulled out the pearl he'd found beneath his desk. He rolled it between forefinger and thumb. "Familiar?"

She shrugged, but he could see the truth in her eyes.

"You're gutsy." He threw the pearl at her, but she made no attempt to catch it. It landed on the chair cushion and rolled to the floor. "I admire that."

"Is that why you set me up so I'd be indicted?"

He shook his head. "Not my doing."

"Like I really have reason to trust your word. *You* came to *me*."

"I was interested in expanding my business outside of Chicago. A friend suggested you might be open to a partnership. You weren't."

"And so you threatened me."

"So, I got a temper."

"And tried to have me killed."

"I don't condone murder." He waited a beat and to scare her added, "Not often, anyhow. Not usually a woman."

"I don't believe you."

"Believe what you want, then."

"This black book of yours...what's it worth to you to get it back?" she asked, coolly seating herself as if she was in a position to dicker.

"Then you got it."

"I didn't say that."

Joey was running out of patience. He had no doubts she and Kaminsky had been in his home the other day. So who else should he look to? He wanted the damned book before it fell into the wrong hands.

"Look, you help me...I help you."

"Help me what?"

"How about stay alive?"

The Dragon woman went unnaturally pale. "Then that *was* your hireling who tried to kill me."

He sighed. "What kinda world is this where a man's word ain't good enough?"

"If it wasn't you, then who was responsible? And don't tell me you don't know." When he remained tight-lipped, she said, "Someone in Las Vegas...Wily."

"Wily." Joey nodded and gave her a wolfish grin. "And where might you have gotten that name?"

Color flushed her cheeks. He had her. Cornered, she went on the offensive.

"How did you know where to find us?"

"Your boyfriend has a big mouth."

"Douglas?"

Who did she think she was kidding? He pulled a face. "The one outside." Suddenly remembering he'd sent Adolpho to fetch the man, he muttered, "Where is he, anyhow?"

"Micah? *He* told you?"

"That'd bother you, wouldn't it?" That she'd fallen for Kaminsky in so short a time wrung a little sympathy from him. He had a feeling that when she knew what was what she wasn't going to be too happy. "Let's say Kaminsky didn't put me onto you directly."

Joey could practically hear her brain computing. He could tell she wasn't certain she could really believe in the man, but she wanted to believe him enough to convince herself...at least for the moment.

Working up some righteous indignation, she asked, "Where the heck are we, anyway?"

"An associate's place in Wyoming."

No sooner had she digested the answer than the name "Frank Gonnella" popped from her lips. "He did set me up, right?''

Not about to give her anything more pithy than a hooded look, he said, "The phone book, missy." When she held fast, he raised his voice a notch. "I ain't playing around here. I mean to get that book back, but I *can't* give you a name in exchange. It wouldn't be healthy for me...know what I mean?"

"Then how are you going to keep me alive? Or do you plan on locking me away, holding me in a different sort of prison than one with bars?"

"I was considering taking on negotiations...*if* you and me can come to terms."

"What's there to negotiate? What does this man want?"

"That's not my business."

"You made it your business when you came to me!" If she had any fear, she was hiding it well. "You think my father will forget about you if something happens to me? Tomas Dragonetti ties up loose ends...*know what I mean?*"

A trickle of sweat started down Joey's spine. "Your old man's outta the business."

"Is he?" Her smile was cold and she held his gaze long enough for that sweat to get halfway down his back. "So what can you do to clear my name, Joey?"

"Not a thing."

"My father won't like that."

She was backing him into a corner. *He* didn't like *that*. The name Tomas Dragonetti was not without consequence, even now. His fingers dug into the rough wood of the chair arms as Joey decided he didn't like her.

About to say so, he lost his opportunity when, again, the door banged open.

This time a nasty-looking Micah Kaminsky filled the doorway.

Kaminsky and the .45 in his hand.

TO MICAH'S PROFOUND RELIEF, Angela popped out of the chair unharmed if a little alarmed. He'd been imagining all kinds of scenarios, none of them good. Thoughts of holding her lifeless body had nearly sent him over the edge. He'd been hard-pressed not to do the bastards responsible for this situation permanent damage. Seeing her intact, he wanted nothing more than to rush to her side and take her in his arms...to protect her...to admit how much he would care if anything bad happened to her...but he needed to keep his wits about him for both their sakes.

Her wide eyes glued to his face made his chest squeeze tight. And when she said breathlessly, "You're bleeding again," he almost imagined she felt something as strong for him as he did for her.

He also suspected he looked even worse than he had earlier. "Don't sweat it. I'm all right." Other than feeling like someone's personal punching bag. He stepped into the room and swung the door closed. "Did he tell you anything?"

"Nothing I shouldn't have," Mariscano said, tone taunting.

"Shut your mouth. I was talking to the lady."

Angela moved closer, her very nearness distracting him.

"Joey claims he didn't set me up and that he didn't try to have me killed," she told him. "He's also willing to provide me with protection in trade for his little black book." Nerves were making her talk a mile a minute. "His men didn't find it, did they?"

"I'd say not. I didn't give them much of a chance."

He'd played dead so convincingly he'd managed to get the drop on the bastards who'd blindsided him. "But we probably should get out of here while the going's good."

"Can't we take him with us for insurance?" she asked, adding in a lowered voice, "Maybe we can figure out a way to make him talk."

"And have kidnapping charges brought against us?"

"Surely you don't believe that."

Taking a look at Joey Mariscano in his city suit, Micah imagined the gold bracelets decorating both hands as designer handcuffs. Jail, that's where the bastard belonged, whether or not he'd arranged the hit on Angela. Only it would never happen, not without divine intervention.

"I wouldn't put anything past a Mariscano," he said.

Mariscano laughed. "And this from a Kaminsky. Rich. Real rich." He was looking directly at Angela when he said, "You're gonna regret this...depending on *him.*"

"I'd regret going to jail more."

"Ask him about his old—"

Micah yelled, "I told you to shut up, Mariscano!" He didn't know whether the crook meant to tell her about his father...or him. "C'mon, Angel." Desperate to get her out of there, he held out his key ring. "Your turn at the wheel."

His handing her the car keys was obviously the right move. She started for the door but stopped to pick up a tabloid from a table. The *Las Vegas Star.* Micah glimpsed a photo of Angela before she pulled it to her breast and faced the crook.

"You're certain you don't want to be more helpful?"

"As certain as you."

She nodded. "If you've been telling me the truth, Joey, I have no reason to turn over the book or any other information I might have about you to the authorities. I only want to be free of this lie. And I want to survive. Stay out of my way and I'll stay out of yours.''

"What about your old man?"

"I'll see what I can do."

Surprised by the pragmatic way Angela had offered the crook a bargain, Micah encouraged her right out the door.

Taking a fast look around on the way to the car, she asked, "Where are they?"

He knew she meant the thugs. "On ice…temporarily. Our friend Joey will find them pretty fast, so we don't have time to dawdle."

He was already wiping his fingerprints off the .45…*just in case.*

"What about Adolpho? The one who grabbed me."

"This is his."

Not wanting a gun in his possession, he wouldn't put it back in the wrong hands, either, so he flung it into the wooded area behind the lodge and sent the ammunition in the opposite direction.

Angela started the T-bird and barely adjusted the seat and mirror before putting the pedal to the metal. The sandy earth whipped dust clouds around them and the car first dug in, then grabbed but fishtailed as if it were on ice.

"Easy," he said, already regretting handing over the keys. "She's a city car, and it might be tricky finding a tow service out here."

"I don't plan on getting stuck."

Angela must have been paying attention on the way into the property, for she made all the right moves to get them back out to a paved road. She waited until they were some distance from the lodge before saying, "You wouldn't think of letting me drive before. Why now?"

He couldn't tell her the truth—that his doing so had been a ploy so she wouldn't ask uncomfortable questions. "That knock on the head had me out for a while."

Raw concern in her voice, she asked, "You think you might have a concussion?"

"Hopefully, no. I mean, I don't think so. But there's also no sense in taking chances."

Thankfully, she accepted the statement without questioning him further.

Getting out of the woods and to a road that went somewhere proved to be a trial-and-error production. Finally they were speeding south, the state road all but deserted. Micah glanced over at the speedometer. His stomach knotted. The digital readout recorded eighty-five.

"You know," he began more casually than he was feeling, "this baby makes it seem like we're going slower than we actually are."

"Uh-huh."

He chose to be more direct. "It's harder to control at this speed."

"Don't worry. I can handle it."

With a grunt, he settled back in the passenger seat. He was sure Angela Dragon could handle anything in the world…with maybe a couple of exceptions, like her father…and his own past.

Since it was already midafternoon, Micah wondered how long they should drive and where to find the safest spot to stop for the night. Anyone looking for them would probably do so on the interstate to Cheyenne. Acting as navigator, he pulled out the road atlas and kept them to fast if less-traveled roads.

He also checked out the tabloid Angela had taken from the lodge.

"Anything interesting?" she asked, sounding calmer than he imagined she really was.

"Other than a reporter, speculating over your where-abouts?"

"They know I'm gone, then. How?"

"A tip from an anonymous source."

One he was more and more certain he knew.

Relieved that they hadn't gotten hold of his mug shot, he read her an edited version of the story, which mostly rehashed the past, but reiterated what he'd seen on the news about the two of them.

"I don't understand why they think we're fleeing to-gether," she murmured. "That's a lousy reporter who can't even identify you as a recovery agent."

Noticing that for once she was using a kinder term than bounty hunter, he muttered, "A reporter who works for a tabloid," and was grateful she didn't start specu-lating.

He decided paging through the newspaper—checking for any follow-up articles—would be wise. While there was nothing more on Angela, he did find something of interest.

"Desert Deals took a full-page ad."

"Obviously Frank Gonnella's not hurting for money."

The advertisement featured a shot of Gonnella him-self, standing before a Joshua tree. And a familiar graphic version of the desert plant with a coyote made up the dealership's logo. Micah closed the tabloid and threw it on the backseat.

When they stopped for gas, he cleaned up in the men's

room, and they came away with colas and candy bars for an empty-calorie lunch.

At least the sugar fix gave them both a boost in energy. Before long, however, Angela was squirming in her seat as if finding it impossible to find a comfortable position. She was also yawning. No doubt all her normal energy had been used up in the altercation with Mariscano and his men. And driving mile after mile through uninteresting flat land whose vegetation was baked yellow by a late-summer sun and lack of rain didn't help. Nothing interesting to look at to keep her awake.

"Maybe I should take over driving," he suggested.

"With a head injury? I don't think so."

"I'm feeling fine."

"Or you could be delusional."

Flashing him a look, she raised both eyebrows, making him wonder if she'd known all along he'd used the head-injury excuse to manipulate her into leaving the lodge.

"We'll have to stop soon, anyway." The sooner the better, as far as he was concerned. "We need some serious food. Besides, neither of us got enough sleep last night."

"When was the last time you saw a sign for a motel?" she asked. "For that matter, when did you last see a sign for a town?"

She had a point. Talk about wide open spaces—Wyoming had more than its share. He could count on one hand the number of vehicles they'd passed going in the opposite direction—and on the other, the ones traveling in the same direction that had passed them as though they were standing still. And this despite the fact that Angela was continuing to test the upper limits of his speedometer.

"We need to stay somewhere tonight," he insisted.

"I can make it to Cheyenne."

He feared she was the delusional one. "Cheyenne might not be the best idea—if they look for us anywhere it'll be there." *They* being any one of several possibilities. He pretended to check the road atlas, although he already knew what he was going to suggest. "There's a state park nearby."

"You can't be serious. Another close encounter with Mother Nature?"

"A much gentler one," he said, hoping he was correct about that. "I'm serious about needing a full night's rest. We can't go on the way we have been. We were lucky to get out of one bad situation today, but should we run into more trouble…"

She sighed. "I know I'm going to regret this."

Her agreement relieved Micah more than he could believe. Not only would stopping this early give them both some well-needed wind-down time, it would delay their arrival in Las Vegas by a few extra hours.

Peaceable hours that he would spend in her company.

When exactly had his attitude changed? Micah wondered. They'd been bound at the hip for what seemed like forever, and yet not much more than forty-eight hours had passed. From the first, he'd been anxious to be rid of Angela. Now the last thing in the world he wanted was to let her go.

Not that he would have much choice, Micah knew. Too many things stood between them. Her fiancé, Douglas, for one. But even if her heart were free…

Angela might be attracted to him. She might even care about what happened to him, a bond having been formed by the danger they'd shared. But if she knew the truth—the whole truth—she would loathe him.

Micah meant to be long gone before he could see that particular expression darkening her beautiful almond eyes.

"I'LL MAKE IT QUICK," Micah promised before slamming the passenger door.

He had insisted on getting the groceries, leaving her alone with the car. And the keys. The ring dangled from the ignition seductively. She could start the engine and drive right off...but to where?

Angela simply didn't want to go anywhere without Micah. Besides, he trusted her.

Trust. The concept was a little less foreign to her now than it had been.

Micah had done that. His rescuing her from Mariscano when he could have gotten away made her believe she could count on him. For once, she didn't feel so alone. And for one night, at least, she would be safe, despite Mother Nature's best efforts. No way would anyone threatening be able to find them so far off the beaten path.

Realizing Micah was taking a bit longer than she'd expected, Angela leaned forward and peered through the windshield and the store's plate-glass windows. She spotted him immediately. He stood close to the front door, a paper sack filling one arm, the pay phone in his free hand.

She started at the unexpected sight. He hadn't said he would be making any calls. Who was at the other end? She figured finding out was about as likely as her learning her name had been cleared while she'd been gone.

Trust, she reminded herself.

Surely he would tell her...

But he didn't.

She waited until he dumped the groceries in the back and himself in the passenger seat. Waited until they were on the road. Until she spotted a sign announcing the state park ahead.

Then she casually said, "You took so long, I thought you were buying out the store." For emphasis, she glanced back at the single bag of groceries.

"Just dinner and breakfast" was all he said.

No mention of the phone call. She swallowed her disappointment, but told herself his not volunteering information didn't mean anything. Perhaps he'd just called her mother again—not that she'd figured out why in the world he'd done so in the first place. Or maybe someone in his own family.

Once inside the park, she took a road that wound upward around a river that had been widened and deepened into a reservoir. The resulting cliffs were striated with red and copper, the setting sun intensifying the colors to a polished glow. Trees hung out over crevices as if reaching to the river below, while the water itself sparkled as if cast with thousands of diamonds. The landscape was as beautiful as both the Badlands and the drive through eastern Wyoming had been harsh. And since it was after Labor Day, visitors were scarce, so they would have plenty of privacy.

Angela could almost pretend the nightmare away.

They staked their claim on a camping area set on a high point of land enhanced by a stone fireplace and shelter that the Civilian Conservation Corps had built in the 1930s. While she carried the bag of groceries to the plank table, Micah dug around in the trunk that seemed to contain a never-ending supply of useful items.

"How civilized," she murmured, setting down the

groceries and having a good stretch. "Too bad a real bed doesn't come with the place."

She'd just realized she'd said *bed*—singular—when Micah said, "You can always sleep in the Thunderbird."

Or in his arms, she thought, at once disturbed and intrigued by the image that idea conjured.

Joining her, Micah unfolded a plastic cloth and covered the table, then produced a candle in a glass holder. The bottle of wine that followed from the grocery bag convinced Angela he was trying to make the evening into something special. She couldn't quite say why she was so eager to embrace the idea.

"Uh-oh, that bottle has a problem." She pointed to the cork as she sat on one of the benches.

"And I have the solution."

With a flourish, he produced a corkscrew from one back pocket and two stemmed glasses from the other.

She murmured, "You've thought of everything." While he worked on the bottle, she began spreading out foodstuffs. Her stomach growled as she looked over the prepared sandwiches, containers of salad and fresh fruit. "Should I put some of this aside for lunch tomorrow?"

"No need. We'll be in Denver by then."

Another state closer to home.

She should be anxious to get back. Having learned all she was going to from Joey Mariscano, she needed to work on Frank Gonnella himself.

Truth be told, she was *still* reluctant to recross the Nevada state line, though she realized her reasons were far more complicated than they had been back in Chicago. Micah-complicated. While he'd vowed to help get her out of hot water, she feared that once he'd made good on the promise he would disappear from her life.

Her chest squeezed tight at the thought. And her stomach knotted.

How would she do without him to challenge her, to get her juices flowing, to raise her temper to new heights?

Micah Kaminsky didn't belong in her life, she reminded herself. But now the insight left her sad.

"To clearing your name." He handed her a wineglass and clinked glasses. "And putting away the bastard who framed you."

"I'll drink to that."

The long swallow splashed into her empty stomach and bounced straight to her head. Maybe that's why she felt so unsettled and empty at the possibility of never seeing Micah again.

As they started eating, Angela couldn't stop herself from watching his every movement. She knew the time she had left to spend in his company was limited. His hands especially fascinated her. Those large hands could be like steel when he so chose but, she suspected, could also be gentle.

Seductive.

Imagining those hands exploring the intimate parts of her body, she gulped a mouthful of wine.

"So what do you think about our dinner reservations?" Micah asked. He was smiling at her, the natural expression playing up his dimple.

"I can't imagine finer," she said, to her own surprise. She'd never been a nature girl. "The decor is glorious. The service sublime. The food gourmet."

He laughed. "You were even hungrier than I thought."

Angela longed to hear more of that laughter. She thought she would never tire of it, not if she heard it every day of her life. At the thought, she found herself wondering what it would be like...living with Micah...spending the rest of her days with him.

Taking another long sip of wine, she marveled at the direction of her fancy.

She didn't even know the man.

Or did she?

Considering the question, Angela admitted she didn't have a handle on the little details. Didn't have a clue as to what his daily life was like. What she did have a grasp on was the important stuff.

Micah was strong, smart, razor sharp. He was also an ethical man who couldn't be bribed. Someone she could count on in tough situations.

He prickled. He confronted. He made her feel so very alive every moment she was with him.

What more did she need to know?

Mariscano's parting shot—that she would regret depending on Micah—still rankled, but considering the source, Angela vowed to put it out of mind.

When they finished eating, Micah suggested they watch the last rays of sunset disappear beyond the horizon. Amazingly, he pulled yet another item from his magic hat of a trunk. While he spread the tarp over a grassy area closer to the very tip of the promontory, Angela poured the last of the wine and joined him.

Handing him the glass, she sat on the ground next to him, stretching out her legs and crossing them at the ankles. A sharp breeze gusted over them, ruffling her skirts. The material fluttered up, leaving her legs exposed to midthigh, but she saw no reason for false modesty. Though she hoped to appear relaxed, in reality raw tension vibrated along her nerves. She had never been so aware of Micah as a man.

She gazed at him through lowered lashes. The wind ruffled long strands of golden brown hair around his face, and the beard growth softened his sharp features. He lay resting on his elbows, his pose defining the musculature of his arms and shoulders. And for a wicked moment she wished she could touch him freely.

Competing with the physical attraction, unanswered questions rose to disturb her. Despite her earlier resolve on the subject, the crime boss's taunt replayed itself in her mind.

And so she really couldn't stop herself from asking, "Why did Mariscano say I'd regret depending on you?"

"He was rattling your cage."

Being so close to Micah was enough to rattle her. Distracted by stray imaginings of what could happen between them if they both let go, she nearly put aside her questions. But, feeling as if she needed something to bring her to her senses, she pressed the issue.

"And his crack about your being a *Kaminsky*...what was that? He said it like the name is notorious."

"Might be—" Micah stretched out on his side and relaxed his top leg so his knee touched her thigh "—in some circles."

While he sounded as if he was joking, Angela had the distinct impression that he really was being evasive.

Too aware of the light touch against her leg, she had trouble concentrating. The gown's skirts shifted and caressed him. There was something so intimate in the picture. With difficulty, Angela forced herself back to her interrogation.

"What circles?"

At first she didn't think he was going to answer. Some fleeting emotion crossed his features, only to disappear as quickly as she'd spotted it.

Then he said, "Admirers…and victims…of Harold Kaminsky."

Victims?

"And Harold would be…?"

"My father. Pop's quite good at what he does," Micah said in a conversational tone, his expression passive. "He's only been caught twice."

Angela sucked in her breath. "Caught…as in doing something illegal?"

Micah nodded. "Somewhere he got the idea that living off other people's money was more attractive than making a living of his own."

"He's a thief?" she ventured.

"I'm afraid so."

His midnight blue eyes searched her face as though he feared she would pass judgment on him for his father's deeds. But she would never do to someone else what others had done to her. And for all his outward bravado, she knew he feared that she might. Something more than simple empathy stirred inside her. A bonding of sorts, Angela thought, recognizing him as a kindred spirit.

She reached out and gently touched his face, fingers prickling against the beard growth. His hand quickly covered hers. The connection complete, for a moment Angela lost her breath. When he lowered his hand to the tarp, he brought hers with it, their fingers lightly tangled together.

"How long have you lived with this?" she asked.

"All my life. What choice did I have? Pop cut his path before I was born."

He said this matter-of-factly as though it didn't bother him. But she sensed he was lying—not to her, but to himself. He'd buried his true feelings. He'd compromised himself so that he could believe it was okay.

That he wasn't angry.

Disappointed.

Left feeling cheated—not of anything tangible, but of the things most people took for granted.

He must really, *really* love his father.

Just as I do, a small voice inside her responded. All those feelings applied to her.

Because Micah had told her his father preferred sweet women with forgiving natures, she said, "I assume your mother knew."

"Practically from the first. And she married him anyway. She didn't like what he did, but she loved *him.*"

"And probably thought she could reform him."

Her own mother had once admitted this as being her fantasy throughout the early years of her marriage to Tomas Dragonetti. With time had come acceptance... something Angela still couldn't achieve.

"A man is what he is," Micah said. "Some things can be changed. But a man's basic nature?" He shook his head. "We have two choices. Acceptance or rejection. Simple."

He'd chosen one path with his father, while she'd chosen the other with hers. But it wasn't simple at all.

Odd pieces of past conversations clicked into place. No wonder Micah always sounded as though he was defending her father. His experience wasn't so different from her own...except he had found a way to come to terms with his family problems, while she had never resolved her own inner conflicts.

Did that make Micah a happier person than she was?

Angela wondered.

And she felt for him.

Stretching alongside Micah, propping her head on her hand, she said, "I've never met a man like you before...someone who can truly relate to me. You understand what I've been through...because you've been there yourself.''

"And I've never met a woman like you before...."

He reached out and smoothed the hair from her face. A thrill rocketed through her. This time, *she* caught *his* hand...and held it...and imagined never letting go.

Through the thickening dusk she stared deep into Micah's eyes, recognizing a longing equal to her own. A longing that included the physical, certainly, but that went beyond something so basic.

The way he was gazing at her...with wonder...with wanting...with love.

Love?

Could it be?

Before she had the chance to speculate further, Micah was kissing her, pushing all other thoughts from her mind. She responded, loving the roughness of his beard growth against her face. Loving his hands running under her skirts and over her thighs. Loving the weight of his body as he shifted and pressed her into the ground.

Loving *him.*

It could be.

She had no experience—not with this kind of emotion. Nothing to compare. She'd never felt this way about another man. Had never before allowed her heart to be in jeopardy.

It had to be.

Wanting Micah seemed so natural, so right. They'd been building up to this for days. The only question was how they had avoided consummating their desire for so long.

Angela slipped a hand between them, fingers cleverly disarming his belt. She slid open his zipper even as he burrowed his hand beneath her panties and urged her to lift her hips so he could remove them. Then he lifted his body slightly, allowing her to expose him.

They touched and kissed and joined. They whispered each other's names followed by words that only lovers uttered. They rocked apart and came together in a joyous blast of sensation and emotion.

Angela had hardly drifted down to earth when Micah flipped to his back, using some effort to bring her with him, because her skirts were trapped by their weight. Still, she shot over him, the quick movement punctuated by a tearing sound as the tangled cloth ripped.

Not caring a whit, she murmured, "I always did like being on top in any endeavor."

A ripple of pleasure shot along her spine as he unzipped the gown, his fingers seducing her back. Freeing her, he covered her breasts with his hands. The sensitive flesh pebbled and she gasped with renewed need too urgent to ignore.

"Now let's do it right," he said softly.

"We did it wrong?" She widened her eyes. "Are you sure?"

"Let me show you."

Thus began a seduction as slow and painstaking as their first coming together had been rushed and impassioned.

Micah pleasured her with his hands and mouth, driving her to new heights of creativity. Angela milked every ounce of feverish pleasure from the experience, for who knew what tomorrow might bring?

Life had taught her to expect happiness to be snatched away from her.

What she didn't know was how.

Chapter Twelve

"Tell me about your fiancé," Micah urged as he zipped up the back of her dress the next morning.

They'd greeted the sunrise with another round of love-making.

"Jealous?" Angela teased, though when she turned around she realized this wasn't something to joke about. His expression was serious. Closed. "Douglas isn't really my fiancé," she assured him, her heart skipping a beat. If he *was* jealous, that meant he really cared. "He's a man I've been dating."

His eyes softened. "For how long?"

"A couple of months."

"Sounds serious to me."

"It's serious *to him*. I think. We never even...um—" she searched for a way to put it delicately "—got really close."

His eyebrows rose. "Not in months?"

"I kept avoiding. Maybe I was waiting for someone special to come along...*and sweep me off my feet*."

Chuckling, Micah slipped his arms around her waist and pulled her to him. Her heart hammered and she wondered if they'd dressed a bit too soon.

"So how special am I?" he asked.

"Fishing for compliments? I thought your ego was as big as—" she glanced over his shoulder and down the reservoir "—as this canyon."

He laughed and kissed her. Then, with an exaggerated groan, he wrenched his mouth from hers. "We'd better have breakfast and get on the road."

Reluctantly she left the shelter of his arms, wishing they could be like any other couple, able to relax and enjoy themselves and their newfound love. But they weren't like normal couples—not with their backgrounds. Thinking that made Angela realize anew how little she knew about Micah's past. Wanting in the worst way to know more about his father, she still hesitated to ask.

While Micah set up the table, she surveyed the mess of her gown. The skirt hung in tatters and one shoulder had ripped out. She made a few attempts to fix things, but only worsened the damage until Micah magically produced a pair of scissors. By the time she was finished hacking, however, the garment was substantially reduced in bulk.

"Free at last," she murmured, sitting down to eat.

"But the results were well worth the wait."

The sparkle in Micah's eyes gave her ego a much needed boost.

"If we'd flown straight back to Nevada, you would never have seen me like this." They never would have made love...fallen in love. At least, she had. "Why didn't we?"

He gave her a sheepish grin. "So I'm afraid of flying. Why do you think I have such an attachment to the Thunderbird?"

Angela had a good, long laugh at his expense.

Breakfast was a quick affair. Then, after making certain they put their garbage in containers and left the site as they'd found it, Micah automatically got behind the wheel.

Figuring she'd play navigator, Angela reached into the back seat for the road atlas that sat on top of the tabloid. She grabbed both.

As they started off, her gaze flicked across the front page of the newspaper and she pulled a face. "Terrible photo of me, don't you think?"

"Maybe you should have one that you like better printed up to distribute to reporters," he said with a grin. "You do own a photography studio now."

"Don't remind me."

Her buying the business that had gotten her into this mess was nothing she cared to joke about.

As they headed out of the park, she scanned the article, then paged through the rest of the newspaper, stopping at the Desert Deals ad. She stared at the black-and-white photo of Frank Gonnella, wondering how a man she'd never even met could put her through such hell. As she was about to close the tabloid on his slimy face, she noticed the dealership's logo directly above its Internet address.

"The Joshua tree and coyote."

"What about it?"

"This drawing is just like the other one—you know, on the piece of notepaper that had your license plate number scribbled on it."

"That graphic is probably pretty common."

Angela's excitement rose. "Not likely that it would be identical, though."

Micah stopped the car and searched through his jeans pockets until he produced the scrap of paper and smoothed it open. Taking the paper from him, she compared the graphic to the one in the newspaper. Identical.

"This makes the connection," she insisted. Finally...*finally* they were getting somewhere. "That means Frank Gonnella is our man."

"Or anyone who has access to his supplies."

"Are you trying to discourage me?"

"I hate to see you pinning all your hopes on something that could be a coincidence."

What a strange thing for him to say...almost as if he knew better. She narrowed her gaze on him but, once more, the truth hid behind the mirrored sunglasses.

"All right," she said. "Let's consider an option. An employee. Wily."

He traded the brake for the accelerator and started off. "Except the receptionist didn't know any Wily."

Pulling the phone book from where she'd stuck it between the console and her seat, she paged to *W* and stared at the entry.

"Wily. No last initial. And there's no other entry like this one. All the others have two initials, with the exception of a few duplicates. Those are distinguished by one of them having a first name," she explained. "So I assumed Wily's last initial would be *W*. But what if Mariscano doesn't know Wily's last name? What if Wily is just an identifier for a hired gun and Mariscano doesn't have anything else on the guy?"

"An identifier or nickname."

"Right. Wily meaning clever..." She knew she was reaching. "As in wily coyote." She ran a fingertip over the coyote part of the logo.

"You may have something there."

"When we get back to Las Vegas we can go straight

to the car dealership. If we ask around, maybe one of the employees can identify this Wily.''

''Why wait that long? When we make a pit stop, we can find a telephone.''

''I already tried the receptionist,'' she reminded him.

Micah's eyebrows lifted over his mirrored sunglasses. ''But I haven't.''

THE CALL TO DESERT DEALS would be the second he would make, Micah decided when they stopped in Cheyenne less than two hours later. Angela would be awhile. Having found a real shopping center, he'd given her one of his credit cards and an hour to do some serious damage buying new clothes. Not that he didn't appreciate her outfit, which currently more closely resembled a sarong than a wedding gown.

He punched in the first number and made his report as he'd promised he would.

All the while thoughts of Angela lingered in his mind.

How she'd gotten under his skin. How he wanted to keep her there. How she would react when she found out.

Signing off, he hung up.

And knew he would tell her the truth himself. Maybe she wouldn't turn against him when she finally knew everything. He had to take the chance—he would do anything to keep her in his life.

He made the second call.

''Desert Deals…where the savings are so hot they sizzle!'' the nasal-voiced receptionist answered by rote. ''Can I help you?''

''I hope so, darlin','' he said in his most charming manner. ''I'm trying to track down a man. An employee.''

"The name?"

"That's my problem. I don't know. I'm not even sure he still works for you."

Sounding as if she were trying to stifle her impatience, the receptionist asked, "What's the nature of your business?"

"Personal. Real personal. It's my sister. This guy left her in a family way, and—"

She cut him off. "Uh, maybe I'd better let you speak to Mr. Gonnella, the owner."

"Wait a minute! Before you do that...is he the kind of man who'd sympathize with Rona's plight?"

Micah silently prayed his sister never heard about this little maneuver—she'd make him pay for using her name in vain.

"I—I don't know."

"You sound like a kind person...what did you say your name was?"

"Gladys."

"Well, Gladys, I trust you'd be sympathetic to another young woman's plight. Rona wants to keep this baby more than anything, but she'll be a single mother...one who doesn't make much money. If I can find the father, I'll make sure that's not a problem. Don't you think a man's obligation is to his child?"

Gladys thought about it for only a second. "Yes, of course I do." She sighed. "My girlfriend was in the same situation last year. Well, she still is because the cad skipped town. All right. I'll help if I can, but without your knowing the guy's name, I don't see how."

"Rona called him by a nickname...Wily."

"Wily? Some woman called recently asking for a Wily."

"My sister," he said convincingly.

"Oh, dear. Well, how would you suggest we start?"

"With your employee directory."

"It's a couple of months old. It's a large dealership. We always have some turnover. He could be long gone by now."

A couple of months ago Joey Mariscano had paid Angela his visit. "But that's when Rona was seeing this man who she said worked for you. That directory should be the one."

"Yes, of course. Can you hold on a second?"

After answering another outside call, the receptionist returned and began reading names to him. Though none sounded familiar, Micah made note of them all in hopes that Angela might recognize one.

"That's it for the sales associates and the mechanics."

She made it sound like the tip of the iceberg. "You have other male employees?"

"Oh, sure. They work in the offices, too. Shall I go through them?"

"Definitely. Rona didn't say what he worked at."

This list was shorter...and one of the names had a familiar ring. He asked about the man. Gladys told him what she knew.

"But's it's as I feared," she went on. "He quit a while ago and I don't have a clue where he headed from here."

"It's a start, Gladys. Thank you."

Hanging up, Micah realized how good Angela's instincts were. And how bad.

"YOU CAN TRY THOSE ON right in here," the saleswoman told Angela, leading her into a short hallway off Women's Sportswear.

The dressing rooms lay in one direction, an office in the other.

A deserted office with telephones, she noted.

"Miss! Oh, miss, I need help now!" a cranky customer demanded from the floor.

"Wouldn't you know it?" The saleswoman sounded as frazzled as she looked. Her skin was damp and blotchy, and three pencils poked out of her hair in various directions. "Shorthanded...the other girl goes to lunch early...and more customers than normal."

Her distraction was undoubtedly the reason she hadn't seemed to notice Angela's unusual appearance.

Angela took the half-dozen hangers from the saleswoman and glanced at her name tag. "Don't you worry about me, then, Thelma. I like taking my time, and I can fend for myself. I'll come find you when I'm ready to buy."

"Bless you."

"Miss, *now!*"

"Coming!" Thelma called, scurrying off.

In the first open dressing room Angela quickly hung the light wool-blend trousers and silk shirts she'd chosen. That she would soon be wearing clean and comfortable clothing thrilled her.

But first...

She made certain the saleswoman was occupied with the cranky customer, then slipped across the hall to call Douglas. And her mother. That way she could both assure her mother she was well and find out what Micah had been up to.

About to pick up the telephone, however, she glanced at the computer screen. Someone had been working the Internet and had left without quitting. The opportunity was too tempting to ignore.

She hesitated only a moment—in which she realized that again she had to be breaking some law or other. Somehow that fact didn't seem important when compared to her freedom. Crossing the line was getting easier and easier....

Angela put her scruples aside and concentrated on recalling the Desert Deals Web site from the tabloid ad; she typed in the address and waited. A moment later she was in.

Frank Gonnella was nothing if not narcissistic. His face practically filled the home page. She spent several minutes searching his Web site. Page after electronic page displayed his merchandise—both automobiles on the streets of Las Vegas and bigger vehicles at nearby recreational areas.

Quickly realizing she'd get nothing of value from the computerized advertisement, she quit the site.

Though she didn't quit the Internet.

Still wanting to know more about Micah's father, she seized the opportunity to do some electronic snooping. With a brother whose life was computers, she'd have had to be pretty dense not to know how to find what she wanted. Using a popular search engine, she requested information on Harold Kaminsky from the Chicago newspapers.

What she got in return was a capsulized history of a nonviolent career criminal who for decades had mostly burglarized homes in Chicago's Gold Coast and North Shore suburbs, interspersed with a couple of stretches in the state pen.

And then she came to the latest article.

A little more than a year ago, a supposedly retired Harold Kaminsky had picked up his old profession and had been caught for a third time…in Las Vegas. He'd been incarcerated in the same prison as her own father.

Facts that Micah had neglected to share with her.

Why?

Remembering Joey Mariscano's warning, she broadened her search on Kaminsky…then narrowed it down once more. Her pulse was racing as fast as her fingers on the keyboard. When the screen changed, she went very still, only vaguely hearing the voice calling from afar.

"Miss, are you still in there?"

What she read shocked her to her very core.

Unable to move, unable to process a thought, Angela was staring at the screen when the voice grew louder.

"You can't be in here!"

As if in a trance, she turned toward the door. "What?"

"This is an office for employees only." The pencils in Thelma's hair vibrated with her outrage. "I—I should call security."

Alarmed by the possibility of official intervention, Angela snapped to. "That won't be necessary. I needed to make an emergency phone call is all."

And almost wished she had. Then she wouldn't know what she knew now.

She stood, surreptitiously allowing her fingers to run over the keyboard and get rid of the information she'd summoned.

"I'm leaving right now. I'm sorry. Really."

She made for the door and pushed by Thelma, her chest squeezed so tight she could hardly breathe.

The saleswoman followed her back onto the floor. "You never did mean to buy anything, did you? I'm going to call security."

"No, that's not true." Panicked, Angela walked faster. "And I didn't do anything wrong," she hedged. At least, not in comparison to what had been done to her.

"Can I get some service?" a young redhead demanded.

"I was here first," an older woman insisted.

"Says you."

The customers distracted Thelma long enough to give Angela the edge she needed to get away.

But to what?

To whom?

A man who'd lied to her?

No, not lied, she amended. Micah had merely skipped over the whole truth.

And after she'd *trusted* him.

Though she could keep herself from running through the shopping center so she wouldn't look guilty of something else she hadn't done, Angela couldn't keep her mind from replaying every moment she'd spent in Micah's company.

Every opportunity he'd passed up to tell her the truth.

She half expected him to be waiting for her at the car, but the Thunderbird stood deserted. A reprieve. Time to think. To breathe.

Her gaze strayed to the trunk.

While Micah had given her the credit card, he hadn't given her keys. That wouldn't stop her now. She looked around for something to use and focused on the nearby landscaping with its craggy rocks, some of good size.

Not caring what any passersby might think, she found the biggest rock she could lift and smashed it into the lock. The alarm went off at contact. The car's lights began flashing. But the trunk didn't release. She tried again. And again. The metal around the lock crumpled until finally it gave and the trunk opened.

"Hey, look at that!" some young kid said.

"Shouldn't we get a cop or something?" another asked.

Angela didn't even glance their way, so focused was she on her quest. This time she didn't care how many laws she had to break!

Micah's magic hat of a trunk was stuffed. She took it all in. Mechanical tools. Electronic devices. Portable computer. Gadgets she'd never before seen, some whose purpose she could only guess at.

Dear Lord, unless she was sadly mistaken, Micah was carrying around every conceivable tool a burglar would need to be successful.

She'd barely processed that fact when a sharp metallic click from behind alerted her. She was no longer alone.

The security guard? A cop? Micah?

"Turn around easy."

Not Micah. She turned.

No uniform, but an impressive-looking gun.

The man holding the weapon on her was so thin as to be bony, with sparse brown hair topping a weasely face.

Sucking in a shaky breath, Angela suspected it could be one of her last.

MICAH HAD BARELY SET FOOT outside the shopping center when he heard the car alarm.

His car alarm!

The distinctive sound put wings to his feet. Far across the parking lot, Angela stood with a slight man before the open trunk of the Thunderbird. Guessing she'd stopped a theft in progress, he wondered why the miscreant hadn't run for cover. And why Angela wasn't seething with fury.

Instead, she appeared frozen, feet rooted to the ground.

Then he saw why.

The man trained a gun on her.

Micah ran faster even as the stranger pulled what looked to be a wallet from his back pocket. Still stiff, Angela took it from him, stared for a moment, then returned it. They spoke as the man replaced the wallet. The next thing Micah saw was him holstering his gun.

Who in the hell was he? Had he somehow fooled Angela into thinking he was all right?

"Angela!"

She spun around, and even from the good distance that separated them, he could tell something was really wrong. And her clothing—she was still wearing what was left of the wedding gown. The stranger touched her arm, and she whirled to follow him, then stopped at a beige sedan parked a couple of spaces down.

"Angel, wait!"

Without so much as glancing his way, she slid into the passenger seat of the sedan and slammed the door. Micah pushed to move faster, but he was nearly spent. He caught up to the car as it backed out of the parking spot. Barely avoiding being hit, he rounded the rear fender and pounded on the passenger window.

When Angela turned to stare at him, he felt sick inside.

He'd never seen her appear so cold, so devoid of emotion. She looked at him as if at someone who was aggravating her...someone she didn't know. Her expression reminded him of the one she adopted whenever the subject of her father came up.

The car surged forward, and for an instant Micah saw behind the cold expression.

For an instant he glimpsed heartbreak.

His own heart thundered painfully. What the hell had happened?

Breath shuddering through him, he raced back to the Thunderbird, intending to follow. But his trunk was a mess and wouldn't close. Quickly grabbing a bungee cord, he was strapping it down and keeping an eye on the sedan's progress toward the exit when two kids approached him.

"Hey, mister, anything missing?" one asked.

The other added, "Want us to call the cops?"

"No. He didn't take anything."

Micah used his remote to open the door and start the engine as he raced to get in.

"Not the man," the first kid said. "The woman."

"You shoulda seen her in action."

Digesting the fact that Angela—not the stranger—had done such heinous damage to his beloved car, he said, "I already have," and jumped inside.

Taking off, Micah prayed that he would have the opportunity to see Angela in action again.

"YOU LED US A GOOD CHASE," said Leon Woerter.

The bounty hunter had shown Angela his identification—something Micah had neglected to do, she now realized—which was the reason she'd agreed to go with him willingly.

"Not me," she said. "Kaminsky."

"Who is this Kaminsky?"

"I wish I knew."

He could be anyone, even the mysterious Wily. He'd been clever enough, fooling her as he had. Had he seduced her so she would never guess he was hauling her back to his boss, Frank Gonnella?

Or had he kidnapped her for ransom, which would be a plausible explanation for his calling her mother?

Whoever, whatever he was, she would have his head once she cleared herself. Glancing in her side mirror, she spotted a familiar dark coupe behind.

Micah was following them!

"You don't intend to drive all the way back to Las Vegas, do you?" she asked tensely.

"You kiddin'? I done enough driving keeping up with you. I already booked us on a flight outta Denver."

"We're flying? Great." She would fly right out of Micah Kaminsky's life. He certainly wouldn't follow her onto a plane, she thought wryly. "But why Denver?" The city was probably an hour and a half's drive away.

"Not as many flights outta Cheyenne, and we'd of had to wait until tonight for seats."

"Then Denver's fine with me."

"I'm glad you're being so cooperative. I was told not to expect anything but a fight."

Which would have been true had she not learned that Micah Kaminsky was a low-down, lying scumbag. A career criminal like his father before him. Like her own father.

"How did you find me?"

"Charlie Hanson got a tip you were in the area," he said of the bail bondsman offering the reward. "A couple of us kept driving around this part of the state. When I spotted the Thunderbird and checked the plates, I parked and waited."

"Who turned in the tip?" she wondered.

"Hanson didn't say."

And what did it matter, anyway? Angela wondered.

Knowing that wouldn't change things. Not how she felt about Micah. And it wouldn't erase his record.

Ten years ago he'd been arrested for burglary. Caught in the act. Sent to the slammer. A six-year sentence with a possible parole after three. And from the evidence in his trunk, he hadn't changed his act. He'd merely gotten better at not getting caught.

And she'd been worried about whether he could get them into Joey Mariscano's house.

If she never saw Micah Kaminsky again, it would be too soon, Angela thought, wondering how long it took a broken heart to mend. Maybe it was time for one of those mother-daughter talks she'd avoided in the past.

Keeping track of the Thunderbird through her side mirror, Angela vowed she *would* get over him.

Even if it took the rest of her life!

BY THE TIME THEY ARRIVED at Denver International Airport, traffic was so heavy that they had lost Micah without Leon's even trying. She wasn't certain the recovery agent was aware of being followed in the first place, and she hadn't been in the mood to inform him. Too depressed to do anything else, she did whatever Leon asked of her as he turned in the rental car and picked up their tickets. Not knowing what else to do with it, he left the handgun in a locker.

"We'd better hurry," Leon urged, "or we'll miss our flight."

They were within sight of the security check before she realized they hadn't actually lost Micah.

"Angel, wait!"

Depression replaced by fury, she turned to see him pushing his way through the crowd.

"I already gave you enough time to tell me the truth

about your past, you...you crook!'' she yelled as Leon nervously tugged at her arm.

"C'mon, Miss Dragon."

But she was just getting started. "You're no bounty hunter!"

"I never said that. Your assumption."

His contradicting her made her madder. "You'd think a man could whisper a few truths while he's making love to a woman, right? But no, I had to find out the truth about you for myself!"

By now, people were stopping to stare at the show she was providing. And Micah had just about caught up to them when Leon pulled her through the metal detector.

"I can explain everything!" Micah insisted from the other side. "Including how you were set up. I know who Wily is."

"I'll bet you do. So explain to them." She pointed the security guards at him. "That man is after me. He may be armed. You have to stop him, please!"

Micah tried rushing through the metal detector anyway. The alarm went off.

She heard him say, "It's only my handcuffs, not a weapon" as she and Leon ran down the corridor.

They arrived at their gate winded. The last of the other passengers were boarding. Stomach knotted, Angela kept watch over her shoulder as Leon presented their passes.

But Micah didn't show. The security guards must have detained him. Good. She boarded knowing that even if Micah was free to do so, he wouldn't follow her if it meant boarding an airplane.

How in the world could she have fallen in love with a grown man who had a fear of flying?

As far as she was concerned, Angela thought, angrily wiping tears from her cheeks, she'd seen the last of Micah Kaminsky.

Chapter Thirteen

"Angela, my love." Douglas enfolded her in his arms and brushed his mustache against her cheek. "Finally, you're safe."

When she'd air-phoned him to say she was on her way home with the real bounty hunter—using Micah's credit card to do so—Douglas had insisted on meeting her plane. She hadn't argued the point.

"Did you get hold of my family?"

Angela had tried to contact her mother and Petra. Unable to reach them, she hadn't had the heart to leave a message on either answering machine.

"I'm afraid not. They must be out for the day."

"Oh."

Leon Woerter cleared his throat. "Uh, Miss Dragon, we gotta get going."

"Of course."

Douglas addressed the recovery agent. "I'll be happy to offer you two a ride to the police station in my limousine," he said, taking something from his pocket and pressing it into the weaselly-faced man's hand. "It'll give Angela and me a few more minutes together."

Woerter surreptitiously checked out the bill and

stuffed it into his own pocket. "I guess that won't hurt nothing."

A few minutes later Angela was tucked in the back of the limousine with Douglas, while Leon rode shotgun with the driver.

"You rented a limo to pick me up," she said in wonder. "Isn't this a little extravagant?"

"Nothing is too much for the woman I love."

Not having such feelings for him, she couldn't meet his probing gaze.

What was wrong with her?

Douglas Neff was good-looking and charming and very, very attentive. He cared for her, wanted to protect her. Besides which, a businessman like Douglas was far more suitable for her than some bounty hunter... correction...burglar.

She didn't know why she had to remind herself Micah Kaminsky wasn't what he seemed to be.

Thinking about Micah made her so upset that she almost missed the man running alongside the limo as it moved off from the curb.

Her father!

His graying hair whipped around his lined face. Expression agitated, he was gesturing wildly. He seemed to be shouting...warning her about something. A panicky feeling clutched her insides when he fell back and bent over as though he was suddenly having trouble catching his breath.

"Wait a minute...my father..."

"So it is," Douglas murmured nonchalantly.

A sense of doom guiding her hand, she reached for the electronic control to open her window. Nothing happened. "This thing is stuck."

"I'll make a formal complaint to the company."

Realizing Douglas sounded rather odd, Angela began to get a bad feeling…as if she were *his* prisoner rather than Woerter's. Her instincts were on alert. Was that her father's warning? If she were to try the door, would it, too, be *stuck?* Not wanting to test it or to make some wild accusation, she grimaced instead and clutched her stomach.

Noting they were approaching a red light, she moaned, "Oh, no…not again."

Douglas frowned. "Something wrong?"

"That garbage Kaminsky was forcing me to eat…it's been making me sick."

As the limousine slid to a stop at the red light, she flipped a hand over her mouth and made a gagging sound.

An alarmed Douglas said, "Don't throw up in here."

He signaled the driver—she heard a soft click—then reached over to open her door.

Angela wasted no time jumping out and making her break. She flew from the limo and onto the sidewalk, where she hoped to have some protection with other people around her. But she'd barely gotten a half-dozen yards before bony fingers clutched her upper arm and spun her around.

Leon Woerter had hold of her with one hand. He indicated the other hidden beneath his jacket. "I wouldn't try anything if I were you."

"You left your gun in Denver."

"And got another one here."

"When? How?"

"From me," said Douglas, appearing on her other side.

Stomach plummeting, she addressed Woerter. "You

don't have to use that, you know. I came with you willingly. I'm still willing to go to the police with you."

Leon looked to Douglas. "What do you say? Should we let her do that, Wily?"

Eyes wide, she turned to the man she thought she knew so well. "Wily? *The* Wily?"

Douglas snickered and leaned so close his mustache brushed her ear. "At your service, darling."

"I don't believe it."

"You probably don't believe I shot at you in Union Station from behind my newspaper, then," he murmured. "Or tried running you down in front of the Target store."

Details she hadn't shared in her phone calls.

Angela went sick inside. Douglas Neff *was* Wily.

What had happened to her good judgment? One man who'd professed to love her and another with whom she'd fallen in love had both fooled her. The only bright spot was that she'd been wrong about Micah—he wasn't the mysterious Wily, and he hadn't been bringing her back to the man who wanted to see her in jail if not dead.

But all those times Douglas had blamed himself for recommending the purchase of Picture Perfect, he'd been secretly laughing at her. Obviously he had been the direct arm used to set her up, and she'd been blind to anything but his charm.

What choice did she have but to get back into the limousine and hope for another break? Her spirits fell even lower when she realized they were heading away from the city, and she imagined being left to die in the middle of the desert.

The thought of death made her think of her family— of her father.

Die...what if her father did?

She couldn't forget the way she'd just seen him: desperate to get to her, then stopped cold by his own physical shortcomings. The remainder of his mortality struck a blow to the invisible shield she'd raised to keep him out. She remembered something Micah had said about her father making a big mistake in judgment when he chose to hook up with the wrong people.

Thanks to Micah, she had to face the fact that, despite everything, she still loved the man she'd shoved out of her life. Not believing her father was evil, she gave Micah's theory credence. No doubt one wrong move led to another until he was trapped....

Even as she had trapped herself.

A quarter of an hour of silence later, they were passing Red Rock Canyon. She turned vacant eyes on its sandstone bluffs painted yellow and red, pink and purple, wondering how much longer she had to live.

Some time later they turned off the main road onto a hard-packed earthen track. Within minutes, the oasis in the middle of the desert came into view. Stands of Joshua trees and what looked like a manicured lawn surrounded a building that was decidedly Gothic in appearance, with several turrets and towers. An iron-barred gate stopped them until the guard checked the limo's passengers. Then he waved them through.

A lump in her throat, Angela broke the long silence. "What does Frank Gonnella have against me?"

Douglas shrugged. "I don't know."

"Then why did he have you set me up?"

He stared at her, his hazel eyes devoid of emotion and beneath the mustache his lips curled into a nasty smile. "I wouldn't want to spoil the suspense."

"WELCOME to the House of Usher."

Ensconced in a thronelike chair in the middle of the medieval-themed great room, complete with armor and weapons and crests, Otto Usher took a good look at his prize. Tomas Dragonetti's daughter appeared battered and broken, exactly as he'd like her father to see her. Only, now that would never happen.

She pulled away from Douglas Neff alias Wily and ventured closer. "I thought you were dying."

"The provisions for my funeral haven't been made yet."

He didn't miss the fire in her eyes—her father's eyes, her father's fire—when she said, "Maybe I can make the arrangements for you."

He laughed. "Ah, not quite beaten yet, I see."

Smirking, he indicated she should sit, but of course she ignored him. The only other person in the room, Neff, took a chair closest to the door, cutting off any possible chance of escape.

"Can I offer you a drink? A last meal?"

She crossed her arms over her chest and loomed over him. "Is this all happening because of my father?"

"What a smart young woman."

"Smarter than you gave me credit for."

"You know nothing."

"I know you were at my father's trial. You were gloating. Happy that he was going to be put behind bars. Is that because you helped put him there?"

His smile faded. "I didn't like your father, either."

She paced before him, looking as if she were restraining herself from doing him bodily harm. Perhaps he couldn't stop her. But Neff would and he'd enjoy it. He liked playing with his prey before devouring it.

"So you were rivals," the Dragon woman said. "My

father's being locked away left you free to pursue whatever interests you chose. Wasn't that enough for you?''

"Your father tried turning his misfortune on me," he informed her. "I escaped prison. My son Norman didn't."

And like a spider building his web, he'd patiently awaited his next turn.

"Is that what this is all about? You're miffed because your bad seed got his? Or because my father got even with you for your providing witnesses against *him?*"

"Clever girl. Your father's sentence was lightened by his helping the state, while my boy is rotting his life away. He'll still be locked up when I die...which *will* be soon enough."

Though evidently his death was not imminent, as people suspected, Angela thought. He still seemed pretty lively.

"And so you thought you'd get a few licks in first. Murder? That certainly will impress your Maker."

"Another death on my conscience?" He shrugged as if there had been so many that one more wouldn't matter. "I didn't mean for you to die. I have nothing against you. I merely wanted your father to suffer over you the way I have over Norman."

"An eye for an eye?" She laughed. "But your precious Norman is alive."

"As would you continue to be if you'd left well enough alone."

"You mean, gone to jail like a good little girl? Not bloody likely."

"Apparently not."

"If I hadn't figured it out, someone would have. Like my father."

His attention was caught by one of his guards standing in the doorway. "Mr. Usher, unexpected company."

"But I am expected," Micah Kaminsky insisted as he pushed his way into the room. "Right, Otto?"

If she were the kind of woman who fainted, Angela thought, Micah's unexpected appearance would be reason enough. Instead, a burst of adrenaline shot through her.

"What are you doing here?" she demanded as the old man waved off his thug.

Micah ignored her. "What about it, Otto?"

"To tell the truth, Kaminsky, I thought you might slink away and take care of yourself."

"But our business isn't finished."

Business? Micah and Usher? Angela was getting that sick feeling again.

"You kept your part of the bargain...as well as you could...given the circumstances," the old man said. "I have the woman. Consider your debt cleared."

Shaking, Angela sank into a chair. Though he might not be Wily, Micah *had* come after her on Usher's orders. That both men she'd gotten involved with had been working toward the same goal took her breath away. Talk about smart women, foolish choices.

Even so, she found her voice. "Great job, Micah. Congratulations. You should be an actor." What was left of her nails dug into the chair arms. "You gave an Academy Award quality performance."

"Angel—"

Cutting him off, she said, "Otto, you have no idea what a valuable tool you have in Kaminsky here. He'd go to any lengths to complete an assignment. Would you like the details?"

"Angel, stop this," Micah ordered.

Furious, she lunged to her feet and faced him. "Stop what?"

"Believing the worst about everyone. I know it looks bad, but you *can* trust me. I meant it when I said I'd help clear your name."

"Trust you?" she echoed, amazed at his audacity.

He gazed deep into her eyes, softly imploring, "Trust me, Angel. I won't let you down."

For a moment the room went still but for the accelerated beat of her heart. She might be in love with Micah, but having made that mistake once, no way could she justify trusting him again. What reason had he given her to do so?

Then again, why would having her trust be to his advantage now, unless he felt something for her....

"How very touching," Douglas said dryly.

The simple comment set off the differences between the two men. Douglas talked about caring but had never done a thing about it. Micah had saved her life more than once. She couldn't for a moment imagine him cooling his heels waiting for long-distance reports while the woman he loved was getting herself deeper and deeper into trouble. What was she thinking... Douglas *was* the trouble.

And Micah was here...almost directly on her heels.

That could mean only one thing. Despite his fear of flying, he'd come to her rescue using the only possible means of getting to her on time. He'd boarded an airplane. *For her.*

Her heart thundered. Praying all the hope she was feeling was reflected in her gaze, she nodded.

"Otto, look," Douglas said, sounding highly amused, "they're not merely lovers in the physical sense They've actually fallen in love with each other."

Micah scowled at Douglas, then addressed the wizened crook on his throne. "You made a big mistake when you pulled my chain, Usher. You made me believe that you and Tomas Dragonetti were best buddies. That you were concerned about Angela for *his* sake. That all you wanted was her back home, safe and sound, before it was discovered that she'd jumped bail."

"And you were willing to believe anything so you could clear your debt to me. We both got what we wanted."

"I don't like being lied to. And no one uses me."

"Your old man used my son."

"Norman chose to protect Pop from that prison gang. If he's anything like you, he had his own reasons."

"He's alive, right?"

"I'm grateful, but not that grateful, Usher. Force my hand, and I'll play on your field. Believe me, you'll lose."

"What is it you want?"

"Let Angela leave here with me."

"Hah! She'll never keep that mouth of hers shut."

"What makes you think I'll keep *mine* shut?"

"What makes you think I'll let you leave?" Usher's smile was ugly. "And your father has another year or so to serve on his sentence. A year is a long time. Anything can happen...."

Angela recognized that Usher was threatening Harold Kaminsky's life. Would he stop at nothing to satisfy his warped thirst for revenge?

"If you let us go willingly, the only charges you may need to worry about will have to do with your setting up Angela," Micah went on, "because we're going to clear her name even if it means destroying yours."

Usher laughed. "Who would believe your word against mine?"

"My word…and Joey Mariscano's."

"Even if Joey knew what I intended, he wouldn't talk."

Seeing where Micah was going with this, Angela joined in. "He doesn't have to. Joey takes notes on everything." She moved closer to Micah. "Every conversation…every telephone call…every inquiry into certain Las Vegas operations."

From Usher's expression, she was certain he was aware of Mariscano's little quirk.

"He'd never turn over his notes, either."

"But his computer is another story," Angela said, even as she scanned the medieval arsenal around them and wondered how long it would take to jump into a protective suit of armor. "Where do you think he stores his records?"

"Which I printed out for myself." Micah whipped the sheaf of papers from one of the larger pockets of his vest and handed it to the old man. "They're in Mariscano's personal shorthand, but that wouldn't be too hard for a professional to decipher. Oh, in case you're wondering, that's just a copy. I personally placed the originals in safe hands. And should anything happen to his daughter…"

"You gave details of my operations to Tomas Dragonetti?" Usher gave Micah a long, cold look. "You've made yourself a deadly enemy."

"Good thing I removed his venom first," Micah said softly. With an expression that would put the fear of God into any man, he added, "Don't make the mistake of underestimating me."

Usher's face reddened. "Get out, both of you!"

"C'mon, Angel."

Needing no more encouragement, Angela turned to find Douglas blocking the way. "Not so fast." He waved a gun at the two of them.

"Let them go," Usher ordered, "or they'll bring down my entire operation!"

"Shut up, old man. If I let them go, they'll bring *me* down, and I can't have that."

"Douglas, surely you wouldn't shoot me after all we've meant to each other," Angela said, so that Micah would know exactly who he was.

Douglas stared at her coldly. "I don't *do* time. Not even for a pretty piece like you."

She sidled away from Micah and closer to Douglas as if realigning herself. "Are you sure I wouldn't be worth it? *He* thought so."

"Angel!"

She spun on her heel, edging a few more inches away from Micah. "Don't Angel me! You got me in this mess, you...you—" she gave him an intense look, hoping he would understand what she was trying to do *"—bozo!"*

Micah took the blow of the dreaded nickname by taking a step back, putting a bit more distance between them. *"I* got you into this?"

"If you had booked a flight back to Las Vegas, my life never would have been in jeopardy." She gazed at Douglas, held his attention. "Would you believe he's afraid to fly? A grown man."

"Hey," Micah said indignantly, "that was between you and me!"

Douglas snickered. "You sure know how to pick them."

"I picked *you*, Douglas," she said, taking a tiny step to his side. She and Micah had danced far enough apart that Douglas couldn't threaten them simultaneously. He would have to choose whom to shoot first. "I was planning on marrying you. I still will, if you want me."

"What is this?"

"I don't want to die." From the corner of her eye she saw Micah tensing to make his move. She had to keep Douglas's attention on her. "A wife can't be forced to testify against her husband. And you'll be *rich*, calling all the shots. What do you say?"

"I say…" Douglas raised his gun. "Forget it!"

Ducking to the side, Angela heard Usher yell, "Not in here!"

Micah was on Douglas even as the gun went off. Angela swore the bullet cut so close it put a new part in her hair. Her hand flew to her head, checking for another bald spot.

The men crashed to the floor, limbs in a tangle. A second shot went wild. Micah smashed Douglas's hand against a heavy mahogany side table. The weapon went flying, Angela directly after it.

Though she hated guns, she knew how to use them and she certainly felt more in control with it in her possession. When the hall door flew open, she aimed at the guard.

"Close the door and go sit by your master like a good dog."

She kept one eye on him, the other on the men trading punches. Considering she had the gun, she probably could stop the fight at any time…but she didn't like being lied to or used, either, and figured they could work out some of her anger for her on each other.

Micah had the advantage of size and strength. He easily used both to send Douglas flying halfway across the room. Having no sense of fair play, however, gave

Douglas a different sort of advantage. He rushed to the wall, where he grabbed a weapon—some sort of medieval ax.

Angela feared she'd made a mistake by letting this go on. "Stop this now, Douglas!"

Good thing she liked the sound of her own voice. No matter that she pointed his gun at him, he went after Micah with a vengeance.

Before Angela could decide what to do next, Micah grabbed a lance and used its length to deflect the blow. Another strike. Micah danced out of the way at the last minute, practically giving Angela heart failure. The blade split a small table in two, drawing an oath from Usher. His own fault, she thought, for keeping the edge so well honed.

When Douglas raised the ax again, Micah followed up with a move so perfect it seemed choreographed. He sent the butt end of the lance into the advancing man's gut. Douglas made a choking sound and dropped his weapon. Micah moved in and aimed again, sending the length of the wood across the other man's chest.

Douglas flew straight back into one of the suits of armor on display, then dropped to the floor, bombarded by pieces of metal crashing down on his head.

Indicating the gun Angela was again holding on Usher and the guard, Micah sucked in long drafts of air. "Thanks for the help."

Throat tight with relief, Angela said, "You did fine all on your own." She wanted in the worst way to throw herself into his arms and rain grateful kisses on his face, but she figured letting down her guard against the crime boss wouldn't be a wise move. "*I* certainly feel better."

Without ceremony, she handed him the gun. Micah's

expression acknowledged the gesture as at once simple and symbolic—her handing him her trust.

Removing the clip from the handgun, Micah faced Usher and indicated the man under the pile of metal rubble. "It would be in your best interests to get him out of town," he said, wiping away all fingerprints from the weapon. "Send him back to wherever he came from before he went to work for Frank Gonnella." He tossed the gun to one corner of the room, the clip to the other.

The old man nodded. "He'll be taken care of."

That sounded like a threat to Angela.

Not wanting clarification on whether it really was, she let Micah push her out of the great room into the foyer. One of Usher's guards opened the front door. Micah's rental car—a sedate-looking sedan—stood directly in front.

When they were both settled inside and on their way off the property, she said, "Nice wheels," and wiggled her butt around in the seat. "And comfortable."

"I'm glad you approve, since I'll be driving it back to Denver to pick up the Thunderbird."

Her heart skipped a beat. "When are you leaving?" she asked in a small voice, not believing that the man she loved was ready to drive straight out of her life and she didn't have a clue as to how she could stop him.

"We have to get you a change of clothes first. I hate to say it, but I'm sick of that dress. I don't think I could stand seeing you in it on another road trip."

Her breath caught in her throat. "You're suggesting I come with you? I'd be crossing the state line. Again." Not that it much mattered at this point, after all the other laws she'd broken.

"I'm leaving this moment. Your father's getting the ball rolling to clear your name even as we speak."

"Oh, my God, my father! Micah, I think he might have been having a heart attack—"

"Whoa. He's fine. Trust me."

Angela did. Implicitly. Still, he had some explaining left. She understood about his obligation to his father. But the rest of his past still bothered her. Never in her life had she thought she'd be involved with a criminal, not with all her hard-nosed views on the subject. And yet, despite his past—despite all the proof in the Thunderbird's trunk—she had a difficult time believing he was the same man who'd lost three years of his life to the penal system.

She waited until they were well on their way to Las Vegas before asking, "Why didn't you tell me you'd served time?"

"At the beginning, it was none of your business. Later, I knew how you felt about your father. I figured you'd turn on me, too."

"And I did."

"Because you found out for yourself. How did you, anyway?"

She winced. "I happened to get my hands on a computer."

"Who ever would have classified a computer as a dangerous weapon?" he muttered. "I meant to tell you, Angel. I just waited too long."

Pulse accelerating with the possibilities, she asked, "You *are* reformed, right?"

"You want me reformed?" He appeared shocked. "I thought you got off on excitement."

"I've had enough for a long, long time." Frowning, she stared at him as if she could climb inside his head. "What really happened, Micah?"

"Good intentions gone bad. My younger brother,

Harry, wasn't a bad kid, but he was always a little squirrelly. He got the idea Pop loved me more than him, so he figured out a way to get the old man's attention. He was going to surprise Pop on a job, help him execute it. I figured it out and went after Harry to stop him.''

"And got caught."

"What was I going to do, turn in a seventeen-year-old who had his whole life ahead of him?''

"You couldn't have been much older."

"Telling the truth wouldn't guarantee I'd get off, anyway. So I served time. No big deal.''

"You're wrong. I can't think of a bigger deal."

And if she hadn't already fallen in love with him...

It hit her then. Another bond. His serving time for something he didn't do—something she hoped wasn't about to happen to her. His fast change of heart toward her made sense. Once Micah believed she was innocent, he hadn't been able to help himself.

"One last thing," she said, hating that she had to ask. "What about that stuff in your trunk?''

When he said, "The tools of my trade," her heart fell. But his clarifying comment—"I'm a security expert"— made it soar. "I learned a lot from Pop, even if I chose not to follow in his footsteps. Not only do I install security systems, but companies hire me to see if I can break through theirs.''

Angela laughed so hard that tears came to her eyes. No wonder he'd been able to get into Mariscano's house and computer. No wonder he was so enamored of gadgetry. As she laughed, she digested exactly how wrong she'd been about Micah. She'd been wrong about a lot of things, but it wasn't too late to start making up for stupid mistakes.

"I've had a lot of time to think about my father over

the past few days," she said. "I want to get to know him before time runs out. I've been using my pride like that armor Usher collects. It got me through some really tough times. It's just that I didn't know when to let it go. I don't want to be like that anymore." Bitter. Isolated. "It won't be easy, but I won't let my pride stand in the way of my happiness any longer."

Micah found her hand and encased it in his own in a firm show of solidarity. "That's great. Tomas is crazy about you."

"How did you get on a first-name basis with my father, anyway?"

"After things started going wrong, I got suspicious of the setup. So I called your father to find out how good a friend Otto Usher was to him. He set me straight."

"Imagine your surprise."

"Imagine. Tomas was instantly ready to send out the cavalry. I assured him I'd take good care of you."

Warmth stole through her as she remembered how well he'd carried through. "A man who keeps his promises." Not to mention proof that her father did love her. "Do you have *any* major faults?"

"I'm sure you'll find every one of them and tell me about them, too," Micah said ruefully. "You know, I'd better call Tomas so he and your mother can stop worrying."

The rental car was equipped with a cellular phone. Micah made the call and offered her a chance to talk to her father herself.

Angela shook her head and said, "I have a lot to say to him. In person."

Micah signed off. "Does that clear up everything to your satisfaction?"

"Not quite."

"What's left?"

"How you feel about me...about us."

"Should I have ridden into the fortress on a white horse?"

"I got the drift," she admitted. "I just want to hear you say the words."

Micah slowed the car and pulled over to the side of the road. He cut the engine and slid closer, so that his magnetic heat surrounded her.

Rubbing knuckles softly against her cheek, he murmured, "I love you, Dragonlady."

"I thought I was an Angel," she complained, her pulse already racing.

"That's before you were willing to let your ex-boyfriend work me over."

"Ever hear of tough love?"

Their gazes locked and Angela was so happy she feared her heart might burst right out of her chest. Micah ran his hand around her cheek to the back of her head. Tangling his fingers in her hair, he pulled her head closer with tantalizing slowness. Then he kissed her. Erotically. Deeply. Stirring her desire for him. More important, her emotions. She'd never felt so close to any human being before. She never wanted the joyful connection to end.

So when Micah released her mouth and pressed his forehead to hers, she whispered, "I love you, too. So what do we do about it?"

He pulled back to look into her eyes. "You want to do something?"

"You doubt it?"

"I wasn't sure I was high-powered enough for you."

Knowing he meant his line of work compared to hers, she purposely misunderstood. "You may be equipped with a little more power than I can handle."

"Good." He grinned. "That'll give me an edge over you."

About to give him a tart reply, Angela stopped herself. Always competitive, she didn't think that would change. But the drive to win every battle was fading. She didn't always have to be first to be satisfied.

"But I'm here and you're there," she reminded Micah of their homes. "And don't say long-distance relationships can work, not when one of us is afraid of flying."

"Who says I'm going to let you out of my sight? Unless I miss my guess, Las Vegas businesses can probably give me more work than I can handle. And considering Usher's threat, I'll feel better being closer to Pop while he's serving out his sentence. You need to be here, too, so that you can work things out with Tomas. Only one thing bothers me. I know you're in the business and all, but do you really have to wear a traditional wedding gown?"

"Are you asking me to marry you?"

"What have we been talking about here?"

Though she hadn't been sure, she didn't hesitate. "Yes!"

"Yes?"

"I'll marry you. And if you're so sick of what's left of this gown—" she gave him an ingenuous look "—you can always take it off."

"Deal," he murmured, his mouth covering hers, his fingers finding the zipper.

Angela settled against Micah, content to let the man she loved take the lead.

This time.

Epilogue

"So they lived happily ever after?" Alex asked when Zoe finished her story and closed the folder on the last of her newspaper headlines: *Dragon Framed, Now Freed.*

Having had a more difficult time reading Alex Gotham's response to the project than she liked, Zoe asked, "You don't care for happy endings?"

"I just don't much believe in them."

Zoe had dealt with more personal disillusionments in her life than she cared to remember, but this might prove to be her biggest professional disappointment. She'd been so certain Alex was right for the project merely from reading his prior work. And now, having met him, she'd sensed a depth in him that convinced her any collaborative effort between them would shine.

She forced a philosophical smile to her lips. "Then writing this book doesn't interest you."

"Wrong. I am *very* interested."

"Enough to put your own prejudices aside?"

"Impossible. But as a writer, I'm also open to other points of view."

"Welcome on board, then."

Standing, she offered Alex her hand. Uncertain exactly where this journey might take them, she surmised it would be a fascinating ride.

Christmastime...

When rediscovering
lost loves brings a
special comfort, and helping
to deliver a precious bundle
is a remarkable joy.

Comfort and Joy

brings you gifts
of love and romance
from four talented
Harlequin authors.

A brand-new Christmas collection,
available at your favorite retail store
in November 1997.

HARLEQUIN®

HARLEQUIN WOMEN KNOW ROMANCE WHEN THEY SEE IT.

And they'll see it on **ROMANCE CLASSICS**, the new 24-hour TV channel devoted to romantic movies and original programs like the special **Romantically Speaking—Harlequin™ Goes Prime Time.**

Romantically Speaking—Harlequin™ Goes Prime Time introduces you to many of your favorite romance authors in a program developed exclusively for Harlequin® readers.

Watch for **Romantically Speaking—Harlequin™ Goes Prime Time** beginning in the summer of 1997.

If you're not receiving ROMANCE CLASSICS, call your local cable operator or satellite provider and ask for it today!

ROMANCE CLASSICS ➞

Escape to the network of your dreams.

See Ingrid Bergman and Gregory Peck in *Spellbound* on Romance Classics.

HARLEQUIN®

I N T R I G U E ®

COMING NEXT MONTH

#441 HER HERO by Aimée Thurlo
Four Winds
Navajo healer Joshua Blackhorse was the one man who could help
Nydia Jim keep a promise to her son—and save a life. But when she
arrived in Four Winds she found Joshua accused of a terrible crime.

#442 HEART OF THE NIGHT by Gayle Wilson
Driven by a need she told herself was professional curiosity,
Kate August delved into the mystery of Thorne Barrington, the only
living victim of a serial bomber. But for what need did she follow him
into the darkness, determined to find the heart of the mystery...and
the man?

#443 A REAL ANGEL by Cassie Miles
Avenging Angels
It was Rafe Santini's job to stop an outbreak of a deadly virus.
Making love to his earthly assistant Jenna wasn't part of his duties. In
all his years as an Avenging Angel, Rafe had never been tempted by
the sins of the flesh. Why now, when so many lives were at stake?

#444 FAMILY TIES by Joanna Wayne
When Ashley's husband was nearly killed, she went into hiding,
taking with her the best part of Dillon Randolph—his baby. It took
three years for Dillon to find her and now he wanted her and his child
to come home to Texas. Surely now it'd be safe to be together
again...or was it?

AVAILABLE THIS MONTH:

#437 FATHER AND CHILD
Rebecca York

#438 LITTLE GIRL LOST
Adrianne Lee

#439 BEFORE THE FALL
Patricia Rosemoor

#440 ANGEL WITH AN ATTITUDE
Carly Bishop

Look us up on-line at: http://www.romance.net

Coming in August 1997!

THE BETTY NEELS RUBY COLLECTION

COLLECTOR'S EDITION

This August start assembling the
Betty Neels Ruby Collection. Six of the
most requested and best-loved titles have
been especially chosen for this collection.
From August 1997 until January 1998,
one title per month will be available to avid
fans. Spot the collection by the lush ruby red
cover with the gold Collector's Edition banner
and your favorite author's name—Betty Neels!

Available in August at your favorite retail outlet.

HARLEQUIN®